L.A. DREAMS

ANTIQUE ASSASSIN BOOK 5

RYAN J. PELTON

PROLIFIC
WRITER PRESS

ABOUT THE AUTHOR

Ryan J. Pelton is a genre-nomad author with over seventeen fiction and nonfiction titles to date. He also hosts a popular writing and publishing podcast (TheProlificWriter.net). Ryan reads, writes, naps, and nurses a Diet Coke addiction, with his wife and four children in Kansas City, Missouri. Find Ryan and his work at: RyanJPelton.com

ALSO BY RYAN J. PELTON

Adult Fiction

Antique Assassin Crime Series

Hired Gun (Book 1)

Stranger Danger (Book 2)

Color Blind (Book 3)

First Blood (Book 4)

Antique Assassin Box Set (Books 1-4)

L.A. Dreams (Book 5)

Stand Alones

The Boardwalk

Watched

Children's Fiction

The Ricky Rayburn Chronicles Series

Secrets of the Ambassadors (Book 1)

Mysterious Pirates of the Pacific (Book 2)

Book 3- coming 2019

Nonfiction

By Way of Reminder

Gospel Driven Leadership

The Gospel Marinated Soul

The Gospel Marinated Life

Gospel Centered Productivity

Everyday Evangelism

40 Days with Jesus

L.A. Dreams by Ryan J. Pelton

Published by *The Prolific Writer Press*, Kansas City, Missouri / www.theprolificwriter.net

Cover by *The Prolific Writer Press*

Edited by Felicity H.

Print- ISBN-13: 978-1-949420-11-1

ISBN-10: 1-949420-11-6

Vanity of vanities, says the Preacher,
vanity of vanities! All is vanity.
-Ecclesiastes 1:2

Talent is God given. Be humble. Fame is man-given. Be grateful.
Conceit is self-given. Be careful.
-John Wooden

"Name for the order?"

"Dexter. Dexter O'Kane."

"Like the serial killer on Showtime?"

"What do you mean?"

"It doesn't matter. Are you going to order or what?" the petite blonde cashier said rolling her eyes.

Dexter adjusted a John Deere trucker hat and the mob of hungry Sushi patrons crowding in on him. Decisions between California or Spicy Tuna Rolls wasn't the same as medium versus well done. Dexter more comfortable with the steak variety.

Noodles Inc. sat on the corner of Pacific and Sunset in Venice Beach California. The restaurant was a popular choice on the boardwalk of the eclectic Southern California beach town. Jake Pope believed Sushi and Raman noodles would be the perfect introduction of big-city-living for the boy from rural Missouri.

Pope was running late and supposed to meet Dexter shortly before noon. Time didn't exist for Pope. Maybe the reason he'd been let go by the Los Angeles Police Department and had to set out on his own, Pope PI Services. The anger didn't help either.

Hoards of Southern California hipsters piled into Noodles Inc. eager to consume overpriced noodles. Their patchy beards and matching flannel staring at their phones like Zombies was worlds apart from LeClaire. A blue collar town of twenty thousand where men had beards, and no man-buns. A dude caught wearing skinny jeans at Rudy's might get a punch in the mouth.

Dexter's stomach churned from the impossible decision over Sushi rolls. What was the difference? How does anyone eat raw fish? Dexter glanced at his watch and avoided the judgment coming from the eyes of the cashier now tapping her fingers on the counter. He imagined a mob of hungry hipsters eating him limb from limb.

"Sir.... Please order, and move to the back of the line. We have a lot of people waiting."

Dexter's eyes glazed over as he spent a moment glancing at the sea of items on the Noodle Inc. menu. Raman, dozens of Sushi items, and strange drinks named Lacroix, overwhelmed his country brain.

"Boston rolls and a Coke," Dexter blurted out. The only familiar ingredient on the roll was an avocado. Something Dexter loved on his burgers in LeClaire.

The waitress nodded and tapped a device on the counter. She flipped the white tablet around and shoved it toward Dexter. "Fourteen eighty three."

"Excuse me?" Dexter asked, playing with some bills in his leather wallet.

"Boston rolls and a Coke... fourteen eighty three," she said, with an annoyed look in her eye.

"I heard you. Avocados wrapped in seaweed, and a Coke. Fourteen bucks?"

She ignored the comment. "You paying with cash?"

"Yeah. Do you have a payment plan?"

"Excuse me," she said, flipping the iPad looking device back around.

Dexter slammed a ten and a five on the counter and sighed. She gave him the change and a plastic cup. Dexter tipped his hat and grabbed the cup playing the events of the day in his overwhelmed brain. His first visit to So Cal had this country boy feeling like a shark flopping on the shores of the Pacific. A fish out of water searching for familiarity. Coke would have to do.

LeClaire had nothing close to what Californians called rush hour. The amount of people and traffic didn't compute for a man raised in wide open spaces. First trip on a plane and first rental car... and first overpriced hipster Sushi joint. Dexter hoped his last.

But the true somersaults in the gut were less about overpriced fish and crowded streets, they were about a girl. Isn't it always? Dexter hoped a few days away from Missouri would allow time for some perspective. Jake Pope offered Dexter a case when family life was on the rocks. Dexter had once again chosen work over family and it bit him in his Missouri behind. Samantha says she left because he doesn't know when to say no. Dexter claimed she didn't understand a cowboy without an off switch. Samantha needed stability. Dexter wasn't in denial. He'd been down this road many times.

Dexter strolled to the back of the Sushi joint. He imagined all eyes on the small town guy. A lost puppy in the hustle and bustle of urban living. He found an uncomfortable metal stool at a high top table in the corner and waited for his overpriced fish. People scurried around the restaurant. Many had golden tans and were glued to their tiny screens in their hands.

80s music thumped through the hipster restaurant and Dexter removed his John Deere hat to take in the scene. The line from the counter a collection of young people, at least young compared to Dexter's aging forty-year-old body. A body beaten down from losing his first wife and kid in an accident. A body beaten down by a second family and a second chance he was squandering in the name of justice. He sipped on the Coke and thought about Samantha and her sweet smile not sure if he'd ever see her again. He also wondered where the hell Pope was. Late, again.

A voice snapped Dexter out of his pity party. The cashier in the front of the store twirled her dreadlocks and hovered above Dexter's Boston rolls. She tried to shout above the chattering in the store. "Number seventy eight. Dexter. Boston rolls... Seventy eight...."

Dexter pointed to his LeClaire Rodeo shirt, waved his hands, and mouthed, "Me?"

The dread-locked cashier nodded.

Dexter dodged a tall Asian kid wearing noise cancelling headphones and oblivious to the world. He bobbed his head, scrolled apps on his phone with one hand, and carried a tray filled with noodles and Sushi in the other. He caught Dexter's eye and gave a look like what planet did you come from?

Dexter made it to the counter, and the cashier wasn't impressed. She stared at the stainless steel counter and reached under. "You want mild or spicy?"

"What?"

"Mild or spicy? For your Sushi."

"How hot is the spicy?"

"It's not bad. But if I were you I'd go with the mild. You know…"

"Know what?"

"You're not from around here. I don't think spicy would fly for someone like you."

The hairs on Dexter's neck stood up and he leaned against the counter. The dread-locked girl finally locked eyes with Dexter. "You think a guy from Missouri can't handle spice? Ain't no way you're going to tell me some hipsters are tougher than me. I'll eat any one of you kid's under the table. You ever hear of cop killer wings, little girl?"

"No."

"That's right. They serve cop killer wings at BB's in LeClaire. Blow your pretty face off. Don't talk to me about spicy."

Eyes were aimed toward the counter as the conversation escalated. "Like, sorry sir," the cashier said, sliding two plastic cups of spicy sauce across the counter. "Spicy it is… Enjoy your food."

A middle aged man wearing a tank top and apparently had spent countless hours working on his biceps gave a smirk. "Don't let these young bucks get you down. Us old guys have to stick together. These Millennials don't know anything," he said, holding out a massive paw. "Roger. Roger Morris."

"Dexter O'Kane."

"What is that? Irish?"

"Yeah, but no accent. Family immigrated many years ago from Ireland."

The buff guy nodded.

The two men strolled to the soda machine and refilled their drinks. Dexter interrogated the mystery man with his eyes.

"Venice is a great place to visit. It'll grow on you. Good people watching," the buff guy said.

Before Dexter could remove the straw from his mouth the mystery man vanished into the crowd.

Dexter didn't dwell on the brief interaction with the buff middle-aged guy because the moans from California hipsters grew inside the crowded store. He blocked a line of people trying to order their food. Dexter's tray of food wobbled as a young girl bumped him. He felt the pinch of his gun pressing against the band of his Wrangler's. He imagined placing a bullet in a hipsters foot.

Dexter lowered his head and avoided the angry mob and forgot about murdering a hipster in broad daylight. He found a seat in the corner. The steam from the Raman noodles fogged his sunglasses. He wiped them down with a rag from his back pocket and examined the plate of food on the table. The food about the same distant from under-standing Missouri and California. Dexter twirled his noodles and sipped his Coke.

The Coke reminded him of John Wood his partner in crime and best friend. Dexter needed to convince Pope that John would be an asset in solving the case. O'Kane was lost and felt vulnerable without John in the big city. No wife and kids didn't help either. John agreed to watch Antique Adventures while Dexter got the low down on the case. Despite John taking a week of personal days the last time he had to run the shop. Dexter wasn't overly concerned. He needed space from all the family drama. John was incompetent, but loyal.

Dexter shook the plastic cup of Coke to get the ice off the side and glanced to the beach through a front window. A man with a dark tan skated by on roller skates and bobbed to music in his ear buds. Kid's no older than fourteen rode unicycles dodging a sea of beachgoers.

A sun beaten man with unkempt hair pushed a shopping cart near the window where Dexter finished the rest of his noodles. He wobbled side to side, and it appeared the weight of the cart was winning. Dexter watched intently and wondered who'd win the battle between man and cart.

The beach bum laid his head against the handle of the cart, mumbled something, and wiped his brow of sweat. Dexter moved on from the shopping cart guy and watched the other interesting people strolling Venice beach. A man painted in silver acted like a robot moving methodically to the watching crowds. A short guy with a Hitler mustache yelled at the sun. Two transvestites roller-bladed in matching purple dresses oblivious to the seas of people walking on the boardwalk.

Dexter paused a beat and took a last sip of soda. The man struggling to push the shopping cart caught his eye for a second time. He wasn't in good shape. Dexter wanted to do something. He played every scenario in his mind of why not? But something about Dexter's Midwest upbringing would not let the man struggle any longer pushing the packed cart across the sidewalk. He tossed the tray on top of the trash bin and exited Noodles, Inc.

Dexter sidestepped the roller skater in the purple dress and wondered for a moment if his trip to LA was a dream. The bizarro world of Venice was part fascination and part terror.

He nudged through the watching crowd. You'd think with the litter of smartphones someone would call for help. Dexter leaned through a crack of people and stared at the homeless guy whose cart was now lying next to him with all his earthly possessions, mostly cans, strewn across the boardwalk. Foam was coming from his mouth and he twitched apparently having a mild seizure.

"Anybody call for help?" Dexter said, fiddling with his phone, and listening for a response. He said it again.

The crowd stared at Dexter like he had two heads and one of them was a Boston roll. A little girl spoke up.

"My daddy called the police."

Dexter gave a half smile to the small blonde girl. She didn't look too concerned about the homeless guy having a seizure.

Jake Pope emerged from the crowd and smiled in Dexter's direction. He pulled him aside and ignored the foaming homeless man.

"I see you've met Charlie. Happens every week. Someone will take care of him. Let's get out of here. We got work to do."

Dexter glanced down at his watch. "You own a watch? I almost had to shoot a hipster in the Sushi joint."

Pope smiled and shook his head. "Venice is nothing like LeClaire. But it'll grow on you."

"So I'm told. Men wearing man-buns, aren't men. That'll be an adjustment."

Dexter's first time in California, and first Boston roll. The spice wasn't a problem.

2

Pope dragged Dexter's body like a ragdoll through the sea of bikers and skaters and sweaty black men playing basketball. Dexter glanced back at Charlie, who was foaming at the mouth. They found a clearing on the Venice Beach boardwalk. An almost bald man hiding his remaining follicles with a classic comb-over stood behind a bicycle with a box attached to the frame. He wiped sweat from his tanned forehead. Pope waved a couple bucks in his face. "Two please."

The man smiled, reached into the metal box, and raised two frozen bananas. Pope handed Dexter the frozen beach treat. "Eat this. Change your life."

The nutty and chocolate coated frozen banana was another first for the Missouri boy. A frozen banana wouldn't stand a chance in the dog days of a Missouri summer.

"What's this?" Dexter asked.

"A taste of California."

"I thought you were sushi people."

Pope licked the banana and shook his head, "That frozen banana will cool down your mouth after the spicy sushi. To be honest, I never understood the appeal of raw fish. Californians are fad chasers, and sushi became a thing a ways back. Food of the rich and famous. An ice cream treat is more my speed. It doesn't discriminate, it's for all people."

"I'd rather have pork. BBQ from Kansas City is an every-man's food. I'd put your rich and famous sushi against a pulled pork sandwich from Joe's KC any day."

"Whatever. You have your opinion, I have mine," Pope said, taking a deep bite into the banana.

"Speaking of food, I enjoyed the spicy Boston rolls. But how does a grown man live off raw fish? I'm still hungry and need more than noodles and bananas on a stick."

"We can eat real food later. We need you acclimated on the case. I didn't fly you out here to be a tourist. It's time to work."

"No hello, how are you Dexter? Right to work, huh? I was hoping to see that Walk of Stars thing."

"You mean the Hollywood Walk of Fame? That's lame. Not as cool as you'd think. Hollywood's riddled with drug dealers and hookers. I'll show you some better spots if we have time."

"Aren't you from So Cal? Isn't the job of the native resi-dent to show off their city? When you came to LeClaire I showed you, well, not much. Rudy's diner has awesome milkshakes."

"True. But when you grow up in a place, you don't act like a tourist. You take things for granted. We don't have time to be tourists now; maybe later if you help me solve the case."

Pope gave a grin with a perfect row of orthodontist corrected teeth, and his sun bleached hair fluttered in the ocean breeze. He looked like Barbie's boyfriend Ken. Dexter had a hard time seeing Pope as the angry type. Never witnessed it in LeClaire. Everyone has their demons and often their hidden behind plastic smiles, or corrected teeth.

Pope ripped into the banana and swallowed hard. "Sorry, Dex, for pressing. I've been working this case since I left LeClaire and need to close up loose ends. It's costing me too much money, and it's kind of personal."

Dexter bit into the frozen banana and an explosion of flavors swirled inside his mouth. People in small town Missouri don't experiment with food or tradition - it's an unwritten rule. "If you're losing money why did you send me that email? Aren't there more competent people in LA to help? I'm not a cheap date," Dexter said, taking another bite of banana before it melted and dropped to the sandy cement.

"People in LA aren't fond of me right now. I've burned a couple bridges. Had to look outside the normal channels of police work."

"Why were you sent to LeClaire?"

Pope hesitated, took a bite, and stared out toward the blazing sun hovering above the ocean. "Let's say I did things my grandma wouldn't be proud of. I broke the cardinal rule of law enforcement."

"My grandma's dead. Enlighten me."

"I broke the rule of all rules. The transgression of all transgressions."

"Left the seat up in the bathroom? Used the wrong rifle during deer hunting season? What, it can't be that bad."

Pope chuckled and tried to hold a piece of banana from falling to the ground, "I wish it was one of those."

"Tell me already. You're paying by the hour."

"I let the work get personal. When those lines blur, nothing good ever happens."

"Isn't it always personal?"

"They train a good cop to separate their personal lives from their work. Hard to do. I got too wrapped up throwing scumbags into jail. Police officers get calloused. A moment of weakness and they snap."

"Come on... Work-life balance is a crock," Dexter said, trying to lighten the mood with a slap on Pope's arm. "You're being vague, spill it man."

"Yeah, we're human. But, I let it get personal and lost my shit."

Dexter gave Pope a look over and didn't see an angry guy between the clear complexion, nice hair, and well-built body. He looked like the average surfer hanging around Venice Beach waiting for the next set of waves. Nothing suggested a man ready to explode.

"What did you do? This is a safe place. I'm an antique dealer from Missouri. My networks are small and selective."

"I hurt someone."

Dexter licked remnants of chocolate and banana from his hands and tossed the stick in the trash. "So... isn't that what cops do? The job ain't saving cats from trees. You deal with the scum of the earth."

Pope stood and paced around in circles like he was preparing a defense in a court of law. "I hurt a dude while off duty. I got caught up in a case and took it too far. Took the law into my own hands."

Dexter waved for more information.

"We worked a case of a child molester. This guy, Jack Barnes, was a school teacher who abused kids at a local elementary school. We had eye witnesses and evidence to put him away for life. He hired a power attorney Reggie Lewis who worked the O.J. Simpson trial in the 90s. He'd done every big case in LA and never lost. Lewis pulled the race card and got Barnes off."

Dexter asked, "Who's O. J. Simpson?"

Pope blinked and didn't respond, staring at Dexter's face like he had grown a second head. "Come on, country boy. Please tell me you know O. J.? The Juice. White Bronco, Al Cowlings, bloody glove... nothing...? Every news outlet in the 90s. First reality TV the world ever saw."

Dexter nodded, "We might have heard something. LeClaire is an isolated place. What can I say?"

"I hope your trip to LA will get you up to speed on the rest of the world. Anyway... I went to Barnes' house and beat the shit out of him on the front lawn. Made headlines in the L.A. Times. Stain on the department. I got probation and transferred to LeClaire. Now they're done with me and think I'm a liability to the department. I wanted to close the case on Barnes and instead got it closed on me," Pope said, slamming a fist into a trashcan, "Sometimes the justice system sucks. We had that bastard. Child molesters shouldn't see the light of day. I wonder why I keep doing this shit when guys like Barnes roam the street free."

Dexter watched Pope shake his now bloodied hand, "There's the rage you talked about. I hear ya, bro. The justice system is great when it works. But it seems it fails many people more often than not. I guess that's why my business doesn't flow through the normal law enforcement channels. Taking the law into your own hands sometimes is necessary," Dexter said.

Pope sat down on a cement bench on the edge of the boardwalk. He flexed the wounded hand a couple times. "Law enforcement is all I know. Only skills I have. If this doesn't work out, I'm a mall cop catching shoplifters at Target, or flipping burgers. I'd rather die."

Dexter slumped on the bench next to Pope. "Here's a weird question. Why did you hire me? An antique dealer from nowhere Missouri who moonlights as an assassin. I'm not exactly the trained professional you need. I don't want to screw this up for you and land you at Target."

Pope forced a smile and rose to his feet. "I've worked with some of the best law enforcement in LA, and some of the worst. When a guy has a natural talent, you see it. You have the it factor."

"It factor?"

"That thing people have. It's not learned in a classroom or by reading books. A person walks in a room and they suck others in. It's like a gift from above. Think of Tiger Woods as a kid. Everyone knew he'd be a great golfer. Tiger got the it."

"Tiger who?"

"Please tell me... it doesn't matter. You got the it factor, Dex..."

"I'm flattered by the compliment, I think. Here to help wherever I can."

Pope squatted in front of the bench. Dexter leaned back and raised his hands, thinking Pope might kiss him. Pope pointed at Dexter's face, "It's in your eyes, man. Those country boy eyes have the intensity of a killer. Sensibilities of a surgeon. You got the it factor, Dex."

"Can you tell my wife?"

"Tell her what?"

"About the it thing. She says the only factor I have is the cowboy factor. Always looking for the next shiny penny, a hill to climb, and a bull to rope. Samantha wouldn't call it, it. She'd say I'm full of shit."

Pope rose to his feet and became animated, like he was preparing for a performance on a stage. "It's like when you're staring down the barrel of a gun and you don't flinch. That it factor when it's the fourth quarter and you're down six and need a touchdown. No fear. Confidence... that intangible stuff. That's the guy I need on my team. It's why I sent you the note and flew you out to this strange place called California."

It flattered Dexter that Pope saw the it. But something confused him - how had he come to these conclusions from a short stint in LeClaire? "You saw all that stuff in me?" Dexter asked.

Pope stumbled over his words and snapped his fingers, "Come, on. When you stood toe-to-toe with that racist Jarrett Stevens. You didn't blink. The Darby kid. You aren't scared of anybody. And you're not even trained law enforcement. LAPD would kill for a guy like you. I've seen guys on the force thirty years not have balls like you."

"Go on."

"And..."

"And, what?"

Pope slumped down into the bench and stared off into the distance. He crossed his legs and tapped the other foot on the boardwalk. "Truth... You're all I got. I need help Dexter, and resources depleted. I'm blacklisted LAPD and only thirty three. You're my last gasp."

Dexter slumped down next to Pope and stared at the clear blue sky. "What is all the it BS? You flew me out here because of the lack of options? Is that what this is about?"

"Not entirely. I'm in a pinch, yes. I don't have many options, yes. But, you're good Dexter, and I've seen you work. We'll make great partners. I need you, brother," Pope said, reaching out a hand.

Dexter grabbed his hand and squeezed, making him grimace. "You know, if my life weren't falling apart, I'd be pissed over the it factor crap. I should be in LeClaire trying to pick up the pieces with my wife and kids. They all need a break from me right now so coming to California is a win-win for all parties. I'll be on the next flight out of this crowded sushi-loving place with any more of your shenanigans. You shoot me straight - that's how I play. I'll do the same..."

Pope fluttered his eyelashes, "I meant what I said Dexter about the it factor. You got it country boy. But I also meant it when I said I've exhausted all my resources. No one wants to touch me with a ten-foot pole. I can't even get a mall cop to help with the case."

Dexter released his death grip on Pope's hand. He relented. "Why do you want to solve this case so bad? What will this prove?"

Pope ramped up his foot tapping and chewed on his nails. "Remember how I said things got personal with Barnes?"

"Yeah. You beat the shit out of a child molester. Is this case related to that guy?"

"This is a different kind of personal. My father is the one I'm trying to track down. He's done some bad things."

A seagull swooped down and gnawed on the remains of a frozen banana swimming in sand and water on the boardwalk.

Dexter nodded. "I'm familiar with fathers in trouble with the law. Tell me more."

3

The wooden steps leading up to Pope's office creaked. Beaten up from the damp weather of Venice Beach. The steps climbed around to a second floor, two-story apartment complex. Stuccoed in some shade of beige. No stucco in LeClaire, Missouri.

Pope had rented the one-room apartment and used it for the offices of Pope PI For Hire. His motto was 'a personal touch on police work'.

Regardless if the motto was true, it was personal. The first floor of the apartment complex happened to be Pope's living quarters. A one bedroom bachelor pad.

Pope jiggled the lock of his office and gave a kick at the bottom of the door. A wooden desk with papers strewn across the top and an outdated desktop computer sat in the corner. Photos tacked on walls and taped to a whiteboard. Dozens of lines and words connecting one another written across the board. Like a psychopath trying to find their next victim.

"You a whiteboard guy?" Dexter asked, examining the poorly written words in black, red, and blue ink.

"Huh?"

"John and I use the whiteboard for all our planning meetings. I like your style."

Pope didn't seem impressed with Dexter's use of a whiteboard. He'd assumed all law enforcement used them. Not to mention schools, companies, and most organizations. Pope tossed his keys onto the desk and slumped into a green leather chair which looked like a thrift store find. Duct tape held the insides of the chair from spilling on the floor.

Dexter said, "From all those photos and scribbles it appears you're getting close to solving the case. What did you discover?"

"My dad's an asshole," Pope said, with folded hands resting against the back of his head.

"Many are."

"Dad was never around. Traveling sales guy who put work before family. Missed most of the big events in my life. He treated my mom like trash. A product of his generation, I don't know. Regardless, not the kind of dad I want to be someday."

Dexter pulled up a metal folding chair and dusted it off, "Parenting's hard. I got three kids of my own. Your dad did the best he could with what he had. My pops wasn't winning any Best Dad of the Year awards. Jailed when I was six for murder and robbery. And I can still do one better."

"Murder and robbery are kind of a big deal. Did he assassinate a President?"

"He killed my mom."

Pope leaned forward in the old leather chair and gave a half-baked smile. "Seriously?"

"As a heart attack. He got caught up with an Italian mob and ended up killing Mom. Talk about assholes... I get it."

"I thought my family had issues," Pope said, shaking his head.

Dexter scratched the side of his face. It confused him why Pope was ranting about his father. "You said earlier the case was personal. Is your dad still around?"

"Yep. He never left. My mom and him are still married and live in LA. Not sure how the marriage survived. Always wheeling and dealing and looking for the next business venture. Recently Dad went missing. Our relationship is still abysmal and I'm not entirely sure why I give a shit."

"Why do you? Let the police find him. You don't owe him anything."

"It's complicated. There's more to the story."

"Why waste your time? If you're over your head, let it work itself out. He's not your responsibility."

Pope paused a couple beats and walked over to the wall of photos. He ripped out the pin holding a photo in place. He tossed it at Dexter. "Any guesses?"

"Looks like Mario from a local pizza shop in LeClaire."

Pope grabbed a second photo and tossed it in Dexter's face, "How about him?"

"Al Pacino?"

"Close. Russian mobsters. Been roaming around Southern California for years. They run an underground crime ring."

"How does this relate to your deadbeat dad?"

"Dad might have been working for these felons. Doing business projects on the side for them. I don't know for sure."

Dexter examined the photos. "Now you have my attention. I have experience dealing with mobs and they're no fun. An Italian mob family in LeClaire almost murdered my entire family and half the town."

Pope snickered. "I see now why you got into the justice racket. Between your criminal father and mobs in LeClaire, it's all clear now. I guess small towns aren't immune to evil, just like big cities."

"Evil is everywhere. Small towns are just better at hiding it because no one expects it. You'd be surprised how much stuff goes down in our small corner of the world. What's the plan?"

"I've run out of good ideas. It's why you're here, Dex. I'm at a crossroads. Every lead seems to go nowhere. I need fresh eyes. Someone to see another angle. Find a clue I'm missing."

"Any hunches of where Dad is? Who might have taken him?"

"Best guess is the Russians. The last business deal Dad did was with some Russian investors. I can't say for sure they'd do anything to him. But remember, my dad's an asshole, and assholes attract more of them. From what my mother told me a lot of Dad's business cronies weren't exactly church going folks."

"You have any contact with these Russian investors?"

"All dead ends."

"Well, I'm fresh meat. These Russians won't know me from Adam. I can do some snooping around. See if we can find your dad?"

"Sounds good. But I have another job."

"Another job? I thought this was your only case."

"Call it a side hustle. Dad's case is pro bono. I need fast cash to keep the doors open. Pay the rent, eat, grown up stuff."

"Please tell me your side hustle is legal. You're not selling weed are you?"

"Weed is legal here."

"Not surprising."

"The side gig's legitimate, I think."

"You think? I don't want to leave California with a record."

"Call it a sting operation of sorts."

"Sounds interesting. Who are you stinging?"

"Some locals. We'll be in and out," Pope said, with a mischievous grin.

Dexter could tell Pope was trying to hide details about the side hustle. "Like thieves stealing old ladies purses on the beach? California gang members? Drug dealers? What?"

"Not exactly. There's a little service I offer clients. They seem to like it."

"Go on..."

"Internet dating is a huge thing right now."

"I've heard."

"These dating sites can attract weird people. Before these couples go on a blind date, they hire me to do surveillance. Make sure their future partner isn't crazy."

"Surveillance? Isn't that illegal?"

Pope waved Dexter off. "No way. I do some looking around. Search a little on the internet. Tap a phone. A room or two. Nothing invasive. People pay well for my services."

Dexter leapt from the chair and took off his John Deere hat. "You're telling me you stalk people before they go on blind dates? People pay you for this?"

"Good money. In the age of social media everyone looks good on the Internet. Everybody's cool and successful online. But when you pull back the curtain what you find is often far from reality. I'm hired to help people find the truth. It's rewarding work," Pope said, with a wink.

"Give me an example."

"I had a guy post a photo on his dating profile of a dead

dude. He must've thought he wasn't good looking enough. Things get wild."

"How do people get away with this?"

"People do stupid things when they're lonely."

"I guess. So what's next? We stalk some poor schmuck at his apartment before he goes on a date? How does this work?"

"Something like that."

"Before we go, can we get some real food? Not sushi."

"I know a good BBQ place we can hit."

"Perfect. I've been thinking about pork all day."

Dexter and Pope ate a giant slab of ribs. Dexter felt full and enjoyed a little taste of home. Everything else until this point had been like living in a foreign country.

———

4

Dexter played with the radio as Pope scoped out some poor sap searching for love. Nothing weird to report except a disproportionate amount of cats in his apartment. Pope wondered if a dude with this many cats was date worthy.

Pope got back into the Honda Civic.

"You enjoy spying like a pervert before someone's first date?" Dexter asked.

"It pays the bills. Ain't cheap living in So Cal."

"So Cal?"

"Southern California. The home of Hollywood and L.A. Dreams. Except no one tells people their dreams come at the cost of loneliness and isolation. Not to mention good weather costs a pretty penny. People do crazy shit for fame," Pope said, firing up the car.

"Is it true all the wannabe actors and actresses work in restaurants and coffee shops? Waiting tables and waiting for their big break? That doesn't sound like a great way to live your life," Dexter said, watching a beautiful blonde girl walk her dog down the street.

"Come on, Dex. It's the selfie generation. Everyone's a brand now. You do what you gotta do to stay afloat. Even if it requires spying on weird dudes with too many cats," Pope said with a grin, as he scanned the city street for an opening to pull out. He kept the car in park.

Dexter felt the separation of California and LeClaire culture. A chasm as wide as the Pacific. Dexter shut off the radio. "Tell me more about the case. I didn't fly two thousand miles to stalk dudes with too many cats. I wanna get to work."

Pope stared out the Honda window, and hesitated with the direct questioning of Dexter. "Ok, you're right, I don't want to waste your time. I never thought I'd be chasing down my deadbeat dad. On one level I hope someone is punching him in the face and humbling his selfish ass. Yet, he's still my dad, and we don't get to choose our families, right?"

"True, I get it. You're torn, been there, done that. You really think I can help out? Sounds like you need a therapist," Dexter said, punching Pope in the arm.

"Hilarious. You're the only guy I know who has dealt with shit like this."

"Criminal fathers? Could write a book about it. You said your pops was in business. You sure he's into some shady stuff?"

"Likely, if the pattern holds true. He's been in and out of the joint for tax fraud. Minor stuff, only did 90 days. Whatever he's into now sounds like he's taking his crime game to another level. These Russians are some scary people."

"My dad killed my mother and robbed a bank. I'm sure I can handle whatever your pops is up to."

Pope reached into the center console of the Honda and

flipped on his phone. He swiped a couple times and handed it to Dexter. "Read the headline."

Dexter mumbled the words. "Your dad's mixed up with a Russian mob?"

Pope shrugged. "That's the word on the street. A couple years ago this gym owner named Roger Morris got busted for tax evasion. Morris was a known millionaire and big-wig in the Venice and So Cal area. When the FBI did some snooping around, they found money laundered to an underground Russian group, called Bratva."

"Was your dad's time in prison connected to Morris?"

"You'd think. It happened earlier. Apparently a weird coincidence. But here's a fun fact: my dad was Morris' accountant."

"You think your old man was cooking the books and working with the Russians?" Dexter asked.

"Maybe. They never tied my dad and Morris to the Russians, just to not paying his taxes. They ended up only paying a hefty fine. FBI is still working on finding out the source of the money laundering."

Pope tossed the phone back into the middle console.

"All arrows point to my dad being involved with these douchebags. After Morris got off with only a fine, my father vanished. If Dad is innocent, running isn't a good look. Where there's smoke there's fire."

"I don't want to be Mr. Obvious. But why in the hell would a rent-a-detective spying on a dating service first date want to get involved with the Russian mafia? Aren't you in over your head? I'm all for helping a friend out but this seems well beyond our pay scale. I thought I'd see some sights, help with a case, and call it a work-vacation. But you got the FBI involved. Why not let the big boys handle it?"

Pope hesitated and Dexter could see the wheels of his mind spinning. "This case is personal."

"You said that before..."

"My mom has a part to play too."

"Your mom's working for the mob?"

Pope wiped a tear from his eye. "No, stupid. She has cancer."

"Oh, man. Cancer's a bitch. Sorry to hear that. My uncle died from liver cancer. How bad is it?"

"She doesn't have long. Dad was the only source of income for supporting Mom. When he vanished, the medical bills racked up. I've been taking every job possible to help out, but it's too much on my salary. If we don't find my dad and figure this out, Mom dies."

The sun set in the distance over the ocean. A beam of light shot through the Honda and blinded Dexter. He held up a hand to shield the piercing light. "Can't we find her some other means of financial help? Tracking down a suspect connected to the Russian mob isn't a wise move. I want to help, but can't you call a rich uncle or something?"

Pope's tears ramped up, and he wiped the side of his cheek with a hand. He reached over to the glove box and used a Taco Bell napkin to finish up. "I'm the rich uncle right now. Most of our family is gone. Why did I ask you to come? You're right... My family's a mess and this is too much for our skill set. We let the Universe, God, or the authorities sort it out. What was I thinking?"

Dexter regretted his comments and knew Pope was too far invested in the case to give up so soon. "You were thinking about your mom. That's what good sons do. It's noble and right. I'm sure she's a great woman, and you'd do anything for her. But the Russian mafia? We had an Italian mob situation in LeClaire once, but that's small town crime.

You don't understand how dangerous these guys are or how deep their networks run. Big city mob shit ain't no walk in the park. I'd like to see my daughters walk down the aisle if possible. You get that, right?"

Pope stared out the driver side window. "You're right, I was selfish. I'm just a small fish in a giant urban pond. In my head, it made sense. I'd track down Dad, get him to pay mom's medical bills, and then let the chips fall where they may. Sorry, Dex, for wasting your time. I'll get you a plane ticket home and we'll call it good."

Dexter shuffled in the cloth seats of the Honda and heard the pain in Pope's voice. The heartache of an absent father was a close companion for Dexter. A dad who tried to live above the law. Dexter's daddy-wound was the reason he still fought crime in the shadows of LeClaire. Evil should be punished and innocent people have the right to live. Maybe that's how Dexter soothes his own conscious?

Dexter slapped the dashboard. "Not yet."

"Not yet, what?" Pope asked.

"I'm in California dammit. In one day I've flown on an airplane, eaten sushi, and seen a homeless guy have a seizure. Stuff not happening in LeClaire. Unless you count Larry Osborne, the homeless drunk who pees on the side of the Wendy's every day at lunch. Let's give it a couple days. Get those bills paid for Mom, make some progress on your dad, sound good?"

"I don't know man. You have a wife and kids. I'm a single dude who's naïve about domestic life. What about Antique Adventures, you probably need to get back? Is John still working with you?"

Dexter smiled. "To be honest, the home front ain't good. Samantha threatened to leave," Dexter cleared his throat, "Make it... she already left and took the kids. John's a big ogre and incompetent, but he is loyal. Antique Adventures will be okay for a few days. I could use a few days to clear my head."

"Samantha left?"

Dexter waved it off. "It'll be fine. We're in a rough patch, every couple has them. I'll call her later and iron things out. I have a way with words."

"That's why I don't have a girl. Our line of work is not conducive for family life. Too much carnage."

"You can do both. But one always seems to win out. Jesus said you can't serve two masters. My master is justice and family always seems to take a back seat."

Pope nodded. "Alright. If you're cool hanging out in the wild world of Venice Beach, I have so much to show you."

Dexter smiled. "Nothing surprises me anymore. Dudes with man-buns took me over the edge."

Dexter felt the Honda shake. A buff and suntanned man in a tank top tapped on the window. He gave the sign to roll down the window.

"Can we help you?" Dexter asked.

"How are you today?" the tanned man said in a calm tone.

Pope leaned across the lap of Dexter and said, "Don't have any money, buddy. Try the Catholic Church up the street."

The man gave a belly laugh and adjusted his sun bleached hair. "I'm not a bum. I wanted to see if I could offer you my services."

Dexter raised his hands. "Sorry guy, we're not those kinds of dudes."

"You're funny. I'm not that kind of guy either. I think I can help you with your situation."

Dexter gave the tank topped man another look. He had a

familiar face, despite most of the people of Venice having tanned and wrinkled skin. He snapped his finger, "Hey, were you in the sushi place earlier?"

The buff guy raised his hands. "You caught me. Yep, that was me. Were those Boston rolls amazing, or what?"

"Not my favorite. More of a BBQ guy..." Dexter said, then realized the situation, "Wait... are you following us?"

"Kind of. Not in a creepy way. I can help you. You're Jake Pope, right? Pops speaks highly of you," Morris said, glancing at Pope in the driver side of the car.

Pope reached for his gun and raised it into the face of the tanned, strong man. "Come again? How do you know my dad?"

The man raised his hands and tried to avoid getting the tip of a gun in his mouth. "Can you please put the gun down? Name's Roger Morris. Your dad was my accountant. He always talked about how proud he was of you. Being in law enforcement and all. That's how I found you. Looked up your Private Investigator business on the web."

Pope kept the gun trained on Morris. "I've never been a dad. But telling your kids you're proud of them to their faces would've been nice. Why should I trust you? From what I know... You don't exactly have the cleanest record. I don't trust people who cheat on their taxes."

Morris stepped back, hands raised, and asked Pope if he could reach into his pocket. Pope obliged.

He handed Dexter and Pope each a business card. It read: Smith and Associates. The same CPA firm Pope's father worked for. "Fair. Yes, I know things look bad. But your dad worked for me and he's a good man. Trust me."

Pope didn't trust his father, but was desperate, and running out of options. His mother wasn't well and money to care for her was drying up. Dexter was on the fence whether to stay in California or head back to Missouri. What harm would it do to hear Morris out?

Pope raised the gun again. "I'm not in a trusting mood right now. But, I'm willing to listen. Where's my father?"

"Meet me at Denny's on Pico and La Cienega Blvd. tomorrow morning seven AM. I'll tell you more."

Pope glanced at Dexter listening intently to the conversation. He peeked at Pope and gave him a nod.

"We'll be there."

Morris thanked them for the time and strolled down the sidewalk, glancing from side to side like someone was following him.

Dexter would be in Venice at least one more day.

5

Dexter and Pope cruised to the Denny's on Pico and La Cienega a few minutes before seven the next morning. Their conversation in the car was minimal before having their first cup of coffee. Dexter watched the cars fly by like sardines in the concrete jungle of L.A. He thought about Pope's mom dying of cancer. This flung his mind to Samantha and his own family. The busy city made the country boy long for home.

"What do you think about this guy?" Pope asked.

"What guy?" Dexter said, his brain not sharp because of a lack of coffee, and being lulled to sleep by the rushing cars on the busy L.A. streets.

Pope slapped Dexter in the arm and readjusted his focus on the road. "The guy we're about to meet. Roger Morris. Can we trust him? I still don't trust guys who cheat on their taxes."

Dexter faced forward in the Honda and peered through the windshield. "One thing I've learned chasing bad guys - they're like those fancy boxes of chocolates you get around the holidays. Most of the candies are nasty. But you get a good one sometimes. People are liars. Occasionally someone tells the truth. We'll see what kind of box we get."

Pope slapped Dexter's arm again.

"What's that for?" Dexter yelled.

"You tell another long ass story again. I send you home tonight. No metaphors before eight."

"Metaphors?" Dexter asked.

"An illustration, word picture. Doesn't matter. My trust meter is low these days. Dealing with shady people most of your career makes you cynical. Not to mention the unreliable doctors, administrators, and insurance people who've been working with my mom. I feel like everyone's a liar."

Dexter thought about Samantha again. "Sorry about your mom. It sounds like this whole situation sucks."

"That's not the half of it. You watch your mom dying of a horrific disease that's eating her from the inside out. And try to keep your shit together dealing with insurance companies that give you the run around. Charging us for stuff they're supposed to cover. Healthcare in America is a joke. Especially if you're self-employed and run your own business."

"You're preaching to the choir, brother. I get hammered every year running Antique Adventures. Four full-time employees and full benefits. My insurance premiums are through the roof."

The Honda eased into a parking spot in front of the Denny's. Pope killed the engine. "Thanks for asking about my mom. Few people are in my corner. Means a lot. For a guy with a rough veneer, you have a good heart, O'Kane."

Dexter waved it off. "Don't get all sappy. You California guys and your sensitivity and man-buns."

"I draw the line with the man-bun. Let's go open the box of chocolates and see if we can find my dad."

The restaurant was full. Roger Morris hovered over an LA Times and sipped a cup of coffee. He glanced up from his paper and called the boys from a booth in the back of the restaurant. "Good to see you boys. I wasn't sure you'd come. If a strange man in a tank top on a city street approached me I'd pass on the offer. Grab a seat..."

Dexter and Pope slid into the red booth. A bubbly waitress with a calf tattoo approached the table with pen and paper in hand. "Coffee, boys?"

"Yes," Dexter and Pope said in unison. The waitress disappeared and Morris folded up the paper.

"Let me get right to it. Your father is underwater and we need to save him. I can tell you where he is but it'll cost you," Morris said, bearing down on Pope.

Pope stood up. "I'm done. You're a scam artist. We give you money and you show us my father. No way in hell. We'll find him ourselves," Pope said, glancing at Dexter looking for support.

Morris held up a hand and tried to calm Pope and told him to sit back down. "Give me a second to explain myself. Your dad's in hot water and we can pull him out. But I need your help."

Dexter said, "Before we save Pope's dad from the Russians and hear you out, we need information; information on you. We ain't jumping into nothing with blind faith."

"Why are you so sure he's connected to the mob?"

"We have our sources," Pope said.

"These people aren't folks you want over for Thanksgiving dinner. They'll end your life and anyone associated with you for looking at them wrong."

"I've had my share of run-ins with scum. Italian mob to name a few. Not our concern right now. We want to know about you, Mr. Morris," Dexter said, sipping on his freshly poured coffee. Pope inhaled his coffee like it was his last.

Morris smiled at Pope, poured a creamer into his coffee, and stirred casually. "No problem. So who am I? Your father and I served in Vietnam together. One night a platoon came out of the bush and opened fire on our battalion. A bullet skimmed my arm. Not a terrible wound, but enough of a scrape that it required medical attention. Your dad bandaged me up and carried me twenty miles to safety. Something about the bond forged in war. We've been friends ever since."

Pope stirred sweetener into his coffee and had a puzzled look on his face. "Dad said nothing about a Roger Morris growing up. He barely talked about Vietnam. Why should I listen to you?"

Morris leaned toward a computer bag lying on the booth. He reached inside and slid a manila folder across the sticky diner table. He nodded at Pope. "Maybe this will change your mind. Open it."

A tattered and faded picture of twelve men in Army fatigues spilled out from the folder. Pope brought it closer to his unshaven face. "That you next to my dad?"

"Yep. And about thirty pounds lighter," Morris said, with a smirk.

"You're in good shape for an old guy," Dexter said.

"Investing in a gym helps. No excuses for not working out when you spend seventy hours a week in the place."

Pope placed the photo back in the folder and slid it back to Morris. "You still own the gym?"

Morris glanced at Dexter and back at Pope. "You seem surprised. So does your dad. He has for years. Your pops is part owner of Goldie's Gym on Sunset and Racine. Spends no time there. But he has his name on the deed."

Pope scratched his head at the new revelations from Morris. It was obvious his story had holes like Swiss Cheese. "Can you give me some context? I got to be honest. Nothing of your story is making any sense. Vietnam buddies. Owner of a gym. I don't have much a relationship with the old man. But why wouldn't he mention this stuff?"

"I'm as puzzled as you. Hurt actually. You only find loyal friends like Jim once in a lifetime. I'm sorry he never told you about me or the gym."

"You never came by the house when I was a kid. I don't remember seeing you around."

Morris shook his head. "Your dad never invited me. He always came to my place. Or we hung out at a bar. He sure could drink."

"Tell me about it. The sauce has done a lot of damage to the family."

"I'm no saint, kid. After Vietnam I had my own demons to deal with. My wife said I was different after coming home. Imagine your own country turning their back on you for fighting a war no one wanted to be in. They were confusing times. Your dad wasn't the only one who liked to drink. If I hadn't found weightlifting and exercise, I'd be in the ground."

Dexter nodded and found the stories of Morris amusing. He had served in the military and could relate with the bond formed in the service. What did the Bible say: a prophet isn't welcome in his home town? "Is that why you bought the gym?"

"Right you are kid. I scraped some money together while working in an ad agency. I wasn't the smartest guy in school. But I could write and create ads for cigarettes and booze. I was no engineer, but it was fun. Once I had some scratch, I asked your dad to be a partner. He refused."

"I thought you said he was part owner."

"He is. But that wasn't until years later. He got married, had you, and some other kids, and worked in sales. I bugged him for years to come and be part of Goldie's and he was always busy with other stuff."

"He sure wasn't interested in his family. We never saw him. Always on another business trip selling shower curtains and bathroom supplies. Later we found out he was banging every girl from De Moines to Denver."

Morris shook his head. He sipped the last drop of his coffee. "I'm sorry your dad wasn't there for you. You think you know someone and they turn out to be monsters. We all have our skeletons in the closet and I don't pretend to be perfect. But there's more to the story..." Morris took a deep breath, "My son works with me at the gym."

Dexter said, "My wife works with me at our antique shop. I can relate. Family businesses can be rough."

"Yeah, good and bad perks," Morris was becoming more agitated with every word. "My son has some problems. I'm not sure how to say this... He might've hurt Jim. I don't know for sure. They've been missing for days."

"Where can we find them?" Pope asked, standing to his feet, "How do you know your son is with him?"

"Danny isn't well. He's been on meds for most of his life. Depression and bipolar. We got in a big fight last week over some issues at the gym. We had words, and he threatened me and your dad."

"What was the fight about?" Dexter asked.

"Your dad isn't around the gym much. But I rely on him to keep our books clean. He does a wonderful job and makes us money. I wanted to give Jim a raise and Danny lost it. He couldn't understand why Jim made more money despite never being around. Danny works his tail off and is underpaid, so he says. I have my reasons."

Pope said, "Why are you paying my dad more? He sounds lazy. I'd be pissed too."

"You're always pissed," Dexter blurted out.

Pope shrugged.

"It's complicated. Last year we caught Danny skimming money out of the accounts. He was using it for God knows what. I should have fired him. But I know because of his mental health issues he's not a find in the job market. I warned him that if he did anything to hurt the gym again, he was out."

"Is Danny wrapped up with the Russians? Paying them money from the gym funds?"

Morris smiled, "You're a smart one. Not an unreasonable conclusion. Danny got into some gambling debts and I think his bookies are Russians. Again, all conjecture."

Morris paid the bill and gave Pope and Dexter a handshake. "A lot to take in fellas. I have another appointment and wanted to lay all my cards on the table. I need you men. We'll be in touch."

Dexter and Pope sat in the Honda and didn't speak. All the information was too much. Even with coffee in their systems.

6

P ope stared at the road with an unrelenting focus and gripped the ragged steering wheel in the Honda. He said little, and all the new revelations about his father weighed heavily on his mind. Despite the heavy meeting with Morris he thought it would be important for Dexter to meet his mother and see her current state of health.

Dexter absorbed the crowded city through the passenger window and wondered how in the world he would survive in the clutches of her grip. How did people live in such overpopulated places? The growth of LeClaire from 15,000 to 20,000 in ten years felt like a boom. Dexter had lived in a small town his entire life. Knew the locals, and their families' families. People were moving out to the far reaches of Kansas City for more land and cheaper housing. He understood... but didn't like it.

Pope said, "Sorry about dragging you into my family drama. Dad wasn't a great guy. But I had no idea he was living a second life."

"Forget it. My family is a cornucopia of dysfunction and

pain. Dad goes to jail, check. Mom marries another guy, he dies of cancer, check. Dad gets out of jail, and wants a relationship with me, check. Then owes some Italian mob guys gambling debts from thirty years ago, check. The Italians want to kill him, and me, check. Don't worry about family drama as mine could have its own reality series."

"Damn. I'll try not to complain about my family. Although a Russian mob might put my family ahead of yours. I'm excited for you to meet my mother. She's about the only thing in my life that's stable. Despite the cancer."

The Honda cruised into the entrance of Palos Verdes Manor assisted living. A nice place butting up against the Pacific Ocean. Pope's father wanted his wife to die in a beautiful place. And to die in luxury carries a high price tag.

A balding man with a pot belly leaned out of the security shack. He gave a wave to Pope. "How's it going kid? Come to see your momma?"

"Yes sir, Raymond. How's your family?"

"Expensive. You'd think retirement would cover my expenses. Still working the security shack to make ends meet. Wife has a shopping addiction. Better than people living in the manor. How's your mom?"

"You know. Good days and bad," Pope said, leaning over to Dexter, "This is my friend Dex. He's from Missouri."

Dexter tipped his trucker hat and gave a wide grin to the security guard. "My lady's good at shopping too. Don't be too hard on her. They keep our lives in order."

"You're right. I shouldn't be too hard on her. Welcome to California. What brings you to La La Land?"

"I'm an actor," Dexter said, trying to hold back a laugh. "No... I'm here to help my friend with a job. Nothing big."

"Have a good time. Don't get into trouble. You might never go home after this great weather we've been having."

"I'll enjoy your humid-less weather for sure. But not your crowds."

"Amen to that. I've talked enough. Go see your momma."

Dexter and Pope waved to the security guard and followed the curved road up to a main lot in front of the entrance. Pope signed in and secured two visitor passes. They took an elevator to the third floor.

"Don't be alarmed. Mom has good days and bad. If she's in one of her moods, she might not be all that pleasant."

Dexter nodded.

Pope gave a gentle knock on Room 307. A frail woman wearing a bandana and flowered sweater peeked around the door. Her cheeks were gaunt and her wrists thin. She gave a wry smile, and it grew with the sight of her son.

"Oh, Jakey. So good to see you. I'm sorry the place is a mess. I didn't think you'd be coming over today."

Pope scanned the room and laughed because the space was much cleaner than his one-bedroom apartment in Venice. No evidence of old pizza boxes from Shakey's or dishes stacked to the ceiling in the sink. The only evidence of uncleanliness was a magazine that had fallen off the coffee table onto the floor.

Pope leaned in for a hug and swallowed the sick body of his mother. "I should've called. But I have a friend in town. Dexter, meet my mom," he said, releasing his mother and ushering them into the small apartment.

Dexter reached out a hand and was rejected by Pope's mother. She pulled his arm into her small frame. "Popes don't shake hands. We're huggers."

Dexter settled into the hug and could feel her bones pressing into his chest. She released him and ushered them over to a couch and an overstuffed chair in a small living area. She shut off the TV.

"You boys want something to drink?"

Pope leapt from the couch and raced to the kitchen. "You sit. I'll make some lemonade. You're in no shape for serving us. We're big boys."

Dexter watched the interaction between Jake and his mother. You could see the love in her eyes for her son and vice versus. He remembered a similar love with his own mother before she died. Not having a father around, and later having a step-father, he never found the same love he had received from his mother. Lois O'Kane was a rock and never stopped helping people until they laid her in the ground. Lois was the only stability in a rocky childhood for Dexter.

Pope's mother settled into the overstuffed chair. "Tell me about yourself Dexter. What brings you to Los Angeles?"

"I'm here to visit your son. We worked together in Missouri last year and he invited me out to see his home. Maybe work on a project together."

"That sounds fun. What kind of project?"

"A work project. I'm in the criminal justice game, like your son."

She sighed, "I wish he'd do something else. Something less dangerous. He was always a great writer. Thought he should go into journalism."

"I heard that..." Pope yelled from the kitchen while he finished making the lemonade.

"A writer? I never knew Jake was a poet?"

"Oh, yeah. He's written poems, stories, and articles for the school paper. I'll show you..."

She left the room and returned with a white cardboard box. "I kept all his stories and poems," she said, spilling them onto the glass coffee table.

Dexter found the trip down memory lane amusing. He

picked up a poem. "I love roses. Violets are better. My mother knit me a sweater..."

Dexter fell into the couch and almost died from laughter. Pope came back from the kitchen with three glasses of lemonade. He handed his mother a glass and placed the other two on the table. "Please stop. I was in the third grade. It's not Emily Dickinson. Give me a break."

"Stick to police work. I think writing might've been the wrong path."

"Let's move on," Jake said, with a roll of the eyes. He sipped on the lemonade and peeked at his mom. "I had an interesting morning. You ever hear of a guy named Roger Morris?"

Jake's mother turned to face a window that overlooked the ocean. A wave crashed below and a flock of seagulls raced through the sky. She sighed, "What did he want?"

"I'll take that as a yes. He invited us to breakfast. Said he was dad's good friend."

"That it?"

"Some other things too. Why? You friends?"

Pope's mother shifted in her seat and didn't answer with words, only a nod. "I'd rather not talk about Mr. Morris. We have a checkered past."

"More than friends? How come I never saw him around the house? Morris said dad and him were best friends. Is that true?"

"They were Vietnam buddies. Roger was obsessed with Jim. Thought he was the best thing since sliced bread. When we got married after the war he became jealous. Thought I was stealing away his best friend. It wasn't true. I had my reasons for keeping Jim away..."

Dexter chimed in, "You kept Jim away from Roger? Why? Was he a bad guy?"

The air left the room and Pope's mom wouldn't look in the boys' direction. She tapped her fingers against the chair and then folded her arms. "I kept Jim away. He wasn't a bad guy. I had different reasons, it's complicated."

Pope said, "Was he going to hurt dad?"

She put her hand on the top of her bandana and placed her pinky in the corner of her mouth. "Well, you know what. I'm dying of cancer and it makes no sense to keep secrets from my family. Roger was not a bad guy. I didn't keep him from your dad because of fear. We had an affair."

Pope raised his hands to his face while knocking his glass of lemonade off the table. "Are you shitting me right now? You were sleeping with another man? Did Dad find out?"

"Yes, years later. I was so riddled with guilt and shame I had to tell him. Roger and I only spent time together for a couple years. But they were some of the happiest times of my life," she said, staring out to the ocean with a smile growing on her wrinkled face.

Pope shook his head, "Is that why dad wouldn't partner with Roger at the gym? Was he pissed you were whoring around with his best friend?"

She shot back, "I'm no whore. Roger and I had something special. We didn't sleep together that much. Our relationship went deeper. Your father was always on the road. I craved the affection of another man. Roger was my soulmate. He paid attention to me. That's all a girl wants. Attention and love. Your dad was lacking in both departments."

Pope went to the kitchen searching for a towel to clean up the spill. He returned and got on his hands and knees and dried up the mess. He glanced at his mother, "This day couldn't be full of more surprises. I meet a guy who's dad's best friend. A guy who I've never met. And find out... you're sleeping with him."

"It was a long time ago. We were young. The sixties and seventies were complex. I'm sure you can resonate with being alone and wanting love."

Dexter resonated as he listened. Samantha came into Dexter's life at the perfect time. She gave the affection and attention he needed. After losing his wife and son to a car accident Samantha was the comfort he sought. It might've been too soon with everything unraveling around his life and business. The thought of divorce was too much. *Love's complex.*

"Yes, I get it. The free love generation and Vietnam were complex times. I want a lover like the next guy. I live in a one bedroom alone and would love to have someone to snuggle at night. But you cheated on dad. That's not cool."

"It wasn't right. My Catholic guilt is strong and not a day goes by when I don't ask for forgiveness. But your dad was not a saint. He treated me poorly and had his own problems with women."

"Did you cheat on dad to get back at him?"

"No. The cheating came later. I think he did it to spite me."

Pope sighed, refilled his lemonade, and took a long sip on the sugary drink. "Let's move on. This is too much for one day."

Dexter pulled out a small notebook from his jeans. "Can you tell us anything else about Roger? We still have some questions about his background."

Pope's mother glanced at Dexter's notebook and thought it odd for a casual conversation. She pointed in his direction. "What is that all about? Is there something I need to know? Is Jim in trouble?"

Dexter scratched his head and stared at Pope. He collected his thoughts. "Does your mom know about your dad?"

"Son, you're scaring me. What's going on?"

Pope took another sip of lemonade and placed the sweaty glass on the table. "You've been going through a lot. The chemo treatments and failing health. I didn't want to add more stress."

"Please Jakey. Tell me what's going on with your father."

"He's missing. And we're afraid he's in trouble. I've been taking care of your medical bills. But sooner or later the money's going to run out. We need his help."

"Jake! You only care that Dad pays my bills. Is that all he's good for? If he's in trouble... shouldn't you care about his safety? He's not been a great father to you and he's been absent in more ways than one. But son, please, can you find him?"

"That's why Dexter's here. He's trying to help me solve a case I've been working on for months. A case that involves Dad."

"Did he do something illegal?"

"I don't want to talk about it. We need more time to make any judgements. But it's looking that way."

Pope's mother reached for the lemonade and it shook in her frail hand. She gasped and tried to find her breath. Pope shot up from the couch and stood in the middle of the living room. "Are you okay mom? You don't look good."

She took one more sip of lemonade and crumpled to the floor. Her drink splashed across the beige carpet.

7

P ope and Dexter rushed to the front desk of the Palos Verdes Regional Hospital. They had stabilized Pope's mother, and she was resting in her room. Severe dehydration was the culprit. Chemotherapy combined with the news about her husband was too much.

Pope chatted with the nurse working at the counter. She sent the boys down the hall and said to make a left. Dexter examined each room as they strolled through the hall. Memories flooded Dexter's brain of when his wife and son were fighting for their lives after the car accident. He had never liked hospitals before the accident and certainly had no affection after the trauma.

Pope waved Dexter to his mother's room.

Before entering, Dexter's phone blew up in his pocket. It was Samantha. He told Pope to go in without him. Dexter found a chair in the hallway.

"I tried calling you earlier today. You didn't pick up. How are things?"

"Sorry, we're busy," Samantha said in a cold tone, "Rosie

had a gymnastics recital and Dexter Jr. had a basketball game."

Dexter held the phone away from his face and tried to hold back tears. Missing the events of the kids was too much. Dexter prided himself on being present with his kids after growing up without a dad. But the sins of the father are too real. Dexter was drawn away from the family because of his side business. He'd discovered a knack for being the hired gun and taking out the dregs of society. The allure was strong and a lot more captivating than he'd ever dreamed. He couldn't stop. Samantha and the kids took the brunt of his obsession with justice. But the thought of never seeing Samantha or the kids again was ripping out his soul. Dexter wiped his face, "How'd Dexter Jr. do in basketball?"

"He had twelve points."

Dexter's face lit up. "That a boy. Taught him everything he knows. Must have his daddy's basketball skills."

"Ain't many Irish men in the NBA."

"How's Molly?"

"She's pulling herself up on the coffee table. Makes for busy days. You doing okay in LA?"

"Had my first Boston roll."

Samantha laughed in the phone. "Sushi? You know nothing about raw fish."

"What about you, country girl?"

"I lived a summer in San Diego with an aunt. Remember, I'm a lot more cultured than you Dexter O'Kane."

"Culture's overrated. Raw fish is expensive. Hoping the job pays well, or I'm gonna go broke. Also can't believe how busy it's here. Never thought I'd be homesick already."

"Take your time coming back. I'm still mad at you."

"Come on baby, I'm sorry. How many times do I have to say it? I promise... last job."

"Dex, I'm tired of words. You've said a lot of words in our marriage and they're empty. It's action and change I want to see. You say you want to be a good husband and father unlike your dad. But when it comes time to choose, your work mistress always wins. I'm preaching to the choir, right Dex?"

Dexter roamed the hallways of the hospital and stared at the floor. He gave an occasional smile to doctors and nurses who were giving him strange looks back. Samantha was right. Work had a stronghold on him like a heroin addict needing a bump.

"I get it, I heard the sermon. But I'm lost without you and the kids. Please let me come home when the job's finished."

"Always when the job's finished. Words. No action. I've heard this sad story more than I can count. You love work more than your wife and this is the bed you've made. Now sleep in it. Do your little case in California and enjoy your mistress."

"That's not fair. I'm only here because you didn't want me at home. I told you I'd stay if you'd have me, but you said no. Give me the word and I'll fly home tonight. Pope can figure things out. Besides, I don't need more raw fish and traffic. I prefer the pace of LeClaire."

"Sometimes life isn't fair Dex. We got together after tons of turmoil. You lost your first family, I lost loved ones. It caught us up in the moment. I knew what I was getting myself into. But now I regret it. You're a good hearted man. But work always wins out. I don't know if I can gamble on you any longer."

Dexter crumbled into a chair in the hallway. He worked hard to not lose his emotions. "I'm not a gamble... I'm your husband. We made vows. Vows that said until death do us part. I'm still here, you're still here. Please

Samantha, I love you, the kids. I can't breathe without you."

Samantha paused a beat on the phone. "I have to go. Dexter Jr. needs something."

"Can I talk to him?" Dexter asked.

"Sorry, you don't have that right today."

Click.

Dexter slumped into the chair and wiped tears from his unshaven face. A rush of doctors pushing a gurney through the sterile hallway breezed past. Dexter imagined lying on the bed with a bright light shining in his eyes. He wanted a second chance on life. Death was a better option than not having his family back. But he made choices. Words wouldn't satisfy Samantha's demands. She wanted to see action and change. But change wasn't possible for Dexter. Caught in the grip of his mistress: justice.

Dexter found Pope's mothers room and snuck into the darkened space. Machines beeped in the quiet room and Pope held his mom's hand next to the bed. "Everything okay?" Pope asked.

"My wife wants nothing to do with me. Other than that..." Dexter said, in a sarcastic tone.

"Bummer. You must've screwed things up bad. I'm no Doctor Phil, but you need to make that right. You lose your family and you lose everything," Pope said, squeezing the hand of his mother.

Dexter found a chair across from the bed. He placed his head in his hands. "You're preaching to the choir, brother. I'm not cut out for family life."

"I'm sure it'll work out. Love always finds a way. Not that I'd know. The other side of my bed is cold most nights."

"I'm selfish for bringing all this drama into your time of need. How's your mom doing?" Dexter said.

"Doctors think she'll be fine. Fluids and rest and she'll be home tomorrow. Other than the cancer, she's doing okay."

"If you don't mind me asking, what kind of cancer is it?"

"A form of CL."

"Plain English please."

"Chronic Leukemia. She's been battling this bitch for a lot of years."

"What's the prognosis?"

"She's at the assisted living facility and kind of just lives with it. Rounds of chemo and radiation. The cancer comes and goes. It's a horrible life. We hope she might leave the facility and live on her own, but it seems unlikely. Unless my dad never comes back and we can't pay the bills," Pope said, with a wink.

Pope's mother gave a slow moan and opened her eyes with a flutter. Pope squeezed her hand and waited to see if she'd wake up. "Mom... it's Jake. You need something?"

She gave out a weak cough and gripped his hand. Her bony fingers were cold. "I'm sorry," she said.

"Sorry for what?"

"For being a whore."

Dexter shot out a laugh and reeled it back in after realizing how loud it was. It reminded him of his own grandma, who always said what she thought and had no filter.

Pope grinned and rubbed the back of her hand. "You're not a whore. We all do stupid things. Your stupid thing was having an affair. It was a long time ago. If I shared every stupid thing I've done, you'd be ashamed to be my mother."

Dexter nodded as he watched Pope and his mother. He knew his life was a bunch of inconsistencies and contradictions. Samantha saw right through his lies and knew it would be a miracle for him to change. Honesty was all Dexter could give Samantha. Even if it stung.

"Oh, honey. I'm so sorry. Your dad was a horrible man. But an affair is never warranted. We made promises to one another to be faithful. I wasn't faithful, neither was he. I kept this secret in too long. It was eating me alive. I'm glad it finally came into the light. I don't have much longer and it's important we keep short accounts. My pastor said that once."

"Mom... you will not die. Stop talking like that. The doctor said you'll be home tomorrow."

She closed her eyes and tears welled up in the corner. "You know this damn cancer will get me sooner than later. I can't take much more chemotherapy or radiation."

"Stop talking like this. I can't lose you too."

She gave a weak wave of her thin hand. "Why do you care? Your father is missing and you only see him as a glorified ATM. Losing both of us wouldn't matter in the least."

Pope released his hand from hers and leaned against the plastic chair next to the bed, shocked at the change of tone in his mother's voice. Mom was always the stable one and dad was the wildcard. Jake lived most of his life with his mother propped up as the hero of the family. Now with the affair in plain view, his mother was no longer the patron saint of his mind.

"I will not hold that comment against you. The medication is messing with your head. Dad's not an ATM. I shouldn't have insinuated that earlier today. I'm stressed beyond my capacity. Without dad in the picture I've been paying your bills. My PI salary is not enough to sustain you for much longer."

"I'm sorry, son. Better if I just died..."

Dexter left the room and allowed Jake and his mother to

work out their differences. He wasn't in the right mind to deal with family drama. Not that he'd be any help, already being an emotional train wreck himself. At least that's what Samantha told him.

One remedy when life wasn't going the way you'd hoped - find a local watering hole and throw down a few. Dexter had his next move.

8

Dexter wasn't ready to visit another hipster joint in So Cal. He wanted a place like Missouri. A bar with common folks and a lot less man-buns. Joe Jost's was just the place. Nothing fancy, beer, pool tables, and normal folks.

Pope said Dexter could take the Honda because he would stay overnight with his mother in the hospital. She was doing a little better and her emotions had calmed down after the crazy day of new revelations and honest confessions.

Dexter straddled up to the bar and popped a pretzel in his mouth. He ordered a Coors and took a moment to breathe and watch the other patrons. No man-buns and flannel. More overweight middle-aged men and a lot of Hawaiian shirts. Apparently another common trend in California, at least among the older Boomer crowd.

The crack of pool balls echoed behind the bar. Dexter turned around to see a slender woman in tight jeans giving him eyes. She moved around the table knocking one ball in after the other. She impressed Dexter with her billiard skills and the God-given shape of her body. A guy in about his late twenties sipped a beer and watched the girl continue to make every shot. Maybe a boyfriend, a brother, who knew?

Dexter turned to the bar and started up small talk with the bartender. He had little margin for error in making amends with Samantha. Despite a nonexistent love life for many months, messing around with a stranger wouldn't be wise. Dexter took a draw on a beer. "How many people live here?" he asked the bartender.

The bartender gave a crooked smile and wiped down the counter with a towel. "Here? Like in Venice, California, the world? Be more specific."

"Venice. I've never seen that many cars and people in one place in my entire life. How do you guys live like this?"

He smirked. "You're obviously not from here."

"What gave it away?"

"John Deere hat. Wrangler's. Your question..."

"That obvious, huh?"

"Kind of. Most locals try not to think about the traffic and the population of California. You live with it and try not to get road rage."

"Road rage?"

"Yeah. Imagine sitting on the 405 freeway in the middle of the day on a Tuesday. No reason for traffic, no accidents, just a sea of cars going nowhere. Now imagine doing that everyday week after week, month after month, and year after year. That would make a man go crazy."

"Damn right."

"So crazy you might lose your shit and gun down someone on the highway."

"No... that happens here? People shooting each other because of traffic?"

"Yep. We call it road rage," the bartender said, placing a

clean glass in a plastic container behind the bar. "Try not to think about the crowdedness. You might not go crazy, brother. What brings you to So Cal?"

"Work. My first time here. I don't get out much."

"Where you from?"

"LeClaire Missouri. Town of 20,000. Most of our town could fit on one section of the freeway."

The bartender laughed. "You're a long way from home. What kind of work you do?"

"It's complicated."

"Is it illegal? You don't appear shady. More like a cowboy. You in the rodeo? I know they got one going in San Bernardino this weekend."

"Been to a couple rodeos in Missouri. Let's say I help people with problems."

"You a therapist? I think those guys are a scam. Pay someone hundreds of dollars an hour to share your feelings. My wife made me go to one when we were having some problems. Better therapy here at the bar."

Dexter sipped his beer and popped another pretzel. "Amen to that. My marriage ain't so good right now. My wife thinks a counselor would help. I'd rather go to Omalley's with my buddies. It reminds me of this place."

"Yeah... sadly, these joints are going away with all the hipsters infiltrating our cities with their over-priced craft beers and food. Bars have no heart these days."

"I've never thought of a bar having a heart. Good way to describe them. Like Cheers used to say: where everyone knows your name. We spend so much time on our phones and driving kids to soccer we barely have time to get beyond the surface stuff. I bet this place has a lot of heart."

The bartender poured a drink for a balding man sitting to the right of Dexter. He slid it across the slick bar top. "It does. The same people been coming here for thirty years," he said, pointing to a man shooting pool in the corner, "That's Mike Young. Been coming here since 1979. A lot more after his wife died five years ago. Therapy, right?"

Dexter nodded. "That's cool. I'm coming around to So Cal. If they have bars like this one I could see myself getting comfortable here."

"I don't know. People are leaving this place in droves. Bad economy. No jobs. High housing prices. Everyone's moving to Texas and the Midwest. So Cal ain't for the faint of heart. I'd considered leaving a few times when the bar wasn't doing good. But we have a loyal community and I don't know where I'd go. My entire life is here."

The woman playing pool asked for another beer. A whiff of flowery perfume punched Dexter in the face. She gave Dexter a glance and stared back at the bartender, who was finishing pouring her drink from the draught.

"Those jeans are tight. Not from around here, are ya?" she said, with a gentle grin.

"I get that a lot around here. Did my lack of man-bun give me away?"

"Something like that. What brings you here?"

"Like here, here. The bar or So Cal?"

"Whatever."

"Work."

"What do you do?"

"I'm an actor. Isn't that what everyone does in So Cal?"

The girl laughed and sipped on her freshly poured beer.

"What's so funny?"

"I'm an actress."

Dexter lowered his head and punched the bar top. He shoved a pretzel in his mouth and tried to remove his metaphorical foot. "I meant nothing by that. I assumed it was a stereotype."

"If something happens more often than not, it's no longer a stereotype. Why would anyone gamble their future on fame and fortune? Answer: crazy people."

"You find fame yet?"

"I'm playing pool in a bar, drinking cheap beer, and talking to you. What do you think?"

"Oh, come on. A pretty girl like you. They'd be stupid not to hire you. Done any movies I've heard of?"

"Not yet. I'm more TV right now. Commercials. They keep the lights on. I'm still pounding the pavement. Something will come along."

Dexter nodded. "I like your positivity. Where does that come from? I could use some perspective."

"Don't know. Life is too short to worry about stupid shit. Hollywood is all about image and hype. I figure just be yourself and what comes, will come. Keep working hard and something good will happen. My perspective isn't religious or nothing. It helps me when things aren't going well."

"Religious or not, I like your perspective. Work hard, don't sweat the small stuff, and good things will happen for you. I will take your advice to heart. Maybe it will help me in my work. Since I'm a struggling actor and all," Dexter said, with a smile.

"You won't get many acting jobs wearing those jeans and that hat."

"Easy. These jeans are ten years old. My favorite pair."

"You must stay in shape," she said, squeezing Dexter's bicep, "Still fitting in the same jeans after ten years. I'm constantly fighting my weight. Always having to be thin for TV parts. It's a weird line of work."

"I bet you've had those jeans a lot of years."

She glanced down. "Don't know. A few years. I could stand to lose a few. Need to lay off the cheap beers. So what do you do for work?"

"I help people solve problems."

"What kind of problems? Getting acting jobs? That would be helpful about now. My commercial gigs are running low."

"I help protect cities from bad guys. I'm like a superhero."

"Come on. Is this a put on?"

"I'd tell you more, but I'd have to kill you."

"Ooh, scary. You don't look so tough."

"I'll tell you what. I saw you playing pool earlier. You have some serious skills. We play a game of eight ball straight up, and I tell you what I do. Deal?"

The girl sipped her beer and took a couple seconds to think about the offer. She nodded to Dexter and within thirty seconds they were breaking serve on a game of eight ball.

A tall and well-built man straddled a high bar chair and watched Dexter and the girl play the game. He was the same guy playing with her earlier. He scowled in the corner, and didn't appear to enjoy the interactions of Dexter and the mystery girl.

Dexter chalked his pool cue, lined up a shot, and fired the cue ball off the three ball. Just missed. The wide shouldered man wearing a plain white tee shirt and skinny jeans snickered at the misfire. "Nice try, country boy," he said, sipping on a Bud Light.

Dexter eyed the girl and looked back at the man who was now standing in front of him. "Got a problem good ole boy? Don't like the way you're looking at her."

Dexter gently placed the cue against the pool table and

gave a smile. "You must be mistaken. I'm no good ole boy. And technically LeClaire Missouri is not in the country."

The warm beer breath of the man wafted in Dexter's face. He recoiled and waved a hand. "Man. You could use a breath mint. Hope you don't plan on kissing your girl tonight before giving a quick brush."

"Hilarious. Be careful what you say. No plans for a fight tonight... but plans change."

"Stop while you're ahead. I don't want you to get embarrassed in front of your girlfriend. She might end up going home with me instead. It would be sad for you to lose your girl to a mere country boy from out of town."

The man placed his beer on a high top table and almost stepped on Dexter's boots. He tapped on his shoulder and whispered. "That girl is my sister. Please stop calling her my girlfriend. She already has a boyfriend, and it's not you. Don't mess with her and don't get hurt. Got it tough guy?"

Dexter backed up and waved his hands in surrender. He reached for the pool cue and lined up another shot. He glanced at the actress. "Your brother? You must be a tight knit family."

She smiled. "I saw the ring on your finger. There's nothing here but some flirty talk and friendly conversation. And what are you... Like forty?"

"Yes. Is that old?"

"I'm twenty nine. Old guys dating young girls in this town is normal."

"None of this matters. I'm a happily married man, or more accurately, still a married man."

"Things not good at the homestead?"

"It's complicated."

Dexter felt a tap on the shoulder. Pope stood in shorts

and a tee shirt and sipped on a beer. "Hey, Dexter. You want to get out of here? You have the car."

"Who's this guy?" the girl's brother asked.

"He's a friend. A single friend," Dexter said, winking at the girl.

The girl gave Pope a look up and down. She liked what she saw. Dexter didn't know if the brother was accurate about the boyfriend, but Pope could use some confidence of late with everything going on in his family. Cold sheets.

The girl and Pope flirted and shot a couple games of pool. Dexter sat on a high bar chair and nursed a Coors. He couldn't believe what was going on in his heart. How close he'd come to doing something stupid with the actress.

Pope took the girl home in the Honda. Dexter took an Uber. His first.

9

Pope stumbled into the living room of his one bed apartment, his hair pointing in every direction. He wore a Pope PI tee shirt and Los Angeles Lakers shorts. Dexter finished a bowl of Frosted Flakes.

"You only eat cereal around here? I tried to find something substantial and only saw row after row of sugary cereal."

Pope rubbed his eyes and grabbed his crotch. "Another reason the ladies don't flock around here like sharks in cold water. And cereal is cheap."

"Where's your lady friend? I heard some interesting noises last night coming from the bedroom."

"You mean yelling, followed by crying, and more yelling. Yeah, that chick was psycho."

"She seemed alright at the bar. What happened?"

"My big mouth got in the way. I was playing Private Investigator...."

Dexter asked, "This isn't some kind of sick dress up game?"

"No... I was asking a lot of questions and her boyfriend

came up. She said they just broke up. How hard it is to find a solid guy. I was tired of hearing about it and she got mad."

"Just like that," Dexter said, sipping the milk from the bowl.

"There's more to it. I might have commented on a heart tattoo she had on her wrist. I said it looked lame. She told me it was to remind her of her dead grandma. That's when the yelling began and the door slammed. All that to say, I slept well... alone. How was the couch?"

"Fine, except it's not made for a full size human. My legs hung off the end. And what's the deal with the loud music in the apartment above you? Do they need to crank Enter Sandman at 2 AM?"

"That's Chico. He works the late shift as a parking lot sweeper. You'll get used to it."

Pope strolled into the kitchen and pulled out a coffee mug. He scoured a cupboard, found a bag of coffee grounds and dumped them into the coffee maker. "You a coffee guy? I can't work without nicotine."

"Work?" Dexter asked, bringing the empty bowl of cereal to the sink. "You think I'm staying in your lovely apartment for fun?"

"Good point. I know things aren't good at home. Where you at with everything?"

Dexter flashed in his mind to a moment in the hospital room with Pope's mother. He saw her frail body in the hospital bed and something clicked inside. Whatever Samantha thought of him and his crazy pursuit of justice at all costs, there was always the human element. He told himself that his drive wasn't for selfish reasons. It was because of people. "I'm in because of your mom."

"Gross, what does that mean?"

"That's not what I mean sicko. When I saw your mom in

that hospital bed, something opened up in me. I'm out here because of what justice represents. The people."

Pope waited for the coffee to finish dripping into the glass decanter. He nodded and scratched his greasy blonde hair. "You might be thinking too deeply about this stuff. I called you because you're the best at finding the threads to solve cases. And I'm in over my head and keep hitting dead end after dead end. Seeing an old friend is nice too because the old apartment is lonely at nights. As you can see…"

"I'm not trying to weird you out. But my wife doesn't understand why I do this side hustle. It's because of people. I hate seeing people suffer and get hurt by psychos and nut jobs. So what we looking at?"

Pope filled his mug, dashed in some cream and sugar, and came and sat on the leather couch. He shuffled some papers on a small coffee table and opened a folder. "Here's what I have so far."

The folder was filled with newspaper articles, website copies, and maps of the city. They were scribbled on with Sharpie like the guy in Beautiful Mind. Dexter picked up an article about a physical trainer connected to some murders. "Who's this?"

Pope sipped on his coffee. He stared at the ceiling and it was obvious he was trying to explain the article, but his mouth was full of marbles. "I mentioned dad might be connected to the Russian Mob. Well, this guy is our target. His name is Boris Popov. Worked at my dad's and Roger Morris' gym. He's a suspect connected to a string of murders. The number is high."

"One thing is certain. He's in damn good shape. Those arms are like my thighs. What do you got on this meathead?"

"Came to So Cal from New Jersey. Supposedly one of the

best personal trainers on the East Coast. Morris recruited him and paid him a lot of money. Goldie's Gym wasn't making money and the hotshot personal trainer would bring in new clients."

"Did it work?"

"Almost too good. Hundreds of people joined the gym. They booked Boris solid every week for his personal training services. They hired a couple more trainers to keep up with the work. But something was odd. Most of his clients were women."

Dexter sipped on a coffee and splashed through the other articles and documents in the folder. "What's odd about that? A good looking young dude from the East Coast. Six-pack abs and big arms. Why wouldn't the women of Venice want to sign up for his services?"

"True. Except he'd only work with women who were aspiring actresses. Young women who wanted to make it big in Hollywood."

"Now you have my attention," Dexter said, holding up a news article from the web, "Is this one of his victims?"

"Don't know. Cops found her under the pier at the beach. She had a Goldie's gym bag and was one of Boris' clients. She was also an actress. The police questioned him and the timeline didn't work. He was home with his wife and kids when the murder happened."

"The beefy man-whore is married? What does his wife think about all the ladies signing up for his services? She must know something is up."

"A few weeks before my dad and Boris went missing, she kicked him out. I think she found something. I've tried to reach out to her with no luck."

Dexter stood and paced around the small apartment. He

scratched his chin and was deep in thought. "What's the Russian connection? You sure the mob's involved?"

"I know you're a country boy and all, but please tell me you know Boris Popov is a Russian name."

"I might've been conceived in an El Camino behind the bleachers at East High but I ain't no dummy. Why do you assume Popov is Russian mob because of his name?" Dexter asked, pouring another cup of coffee in the kitchen.

"Good point country boy. You never want to jump to conclusions when working a case. But when Boris' Russian family came around the gym and moved into the area, we had a hunch. And when my dad had some gambling debts and the Russian bookie threatened to break his legs, we were even more convinced. We are certain Boris is part of something shady out here in So Cal."

"Your dad has a gambling problem?"

"Yep. He's not exactly a front runner for the citizen of the year. The only reason I give a shit about finding him, okay, he's my dad. But I do it for mom too. They're still married, and he has money to help her with treatments. If the Russians punched him a couple times in the mouth and broke his legs. I'd be okay with it."

Dexter shook his head. "Come on now. Be nice, he's still your dad."

"I didn't say kill him. Just mess him up. He needs to be humbled."

Dexter found a notepad and grabbed a pen from the coffee table. He made some notes. "Russian meathead moves to So Cal to work at Goldie's. He's married and has kids. All his clients are aspiring actresses. One is dead. Your dad and meathead are missing. Maybe the Russian mob's involved? About right?"

Pope nodded. "That's where I'm stuck. And all I care

about is getting dad back and seeing mom get better. If this guy is part of a Russian ploy to hurt more people, someone must stop them. What are you thinking?"

Dexter plopped into a chair across from the couch. He shook his head. "I know the home front is falling apart back in Missouri. Everything in me wants to go home. But you're working on fumes. Next stop is Boris' wife. Where can we find her?"

"Manhattan Beach, The Strand," Pope said, "Good luck securing a meeting."

Dexter finished his coffee. "City people find country boys charming. Watch and be amazed."

10

Dexter and Pope made the ten mile drive in the Honda from Venice to Manhattan Beach. Manhattan has the most expensive real estate in So Cal, with the average home price ranging upwards of a million dollars. The Popov compound was no exception.

Dexter's mouth hung open as they pulled into the circular drive of a white mansion. A Ferrari and Jaguar sat gleaming in the midday So Cal sun. "That can't be their house? The largest house in LeClaire could fit in the garage. Is that a five-car garage?"

Pope killed the ignition and made a deep sigh. "Popov was doing well at the gym. Charging premium prices because he could. But this house is ridiculous. No way he was pulling in that kind of cash. I researched the property, and it priced at seven million. That's a lot of scratch for helping ladies tone their buns."

Dexter smirked and stared out the window at two white pillars climbing to the roof line. "Boris is doing well. But my question is how could a bunch of aspiring actresses afford his services? No way they're funding this palace. Russian money? What do you think?"

Pope nodded and was impressed with the good ole boy's attention to detail. It was something he noticed when he worked that stint in LeClaire the year before. Dexter wasn't a trained cop or law enforcement but had the *it factor*. Tuned into every case they worked. Another reason he wanted Dexter in California.

"Goldie's has been doing good. Making this kind of money in two years is absurd," Pope said.

Dexter and Pope exited the Honda and scanned the property. The ocean breeze whipped up and the salty air blew through Dexter's trucker hat. "Don't like your traffic and crowds. I could get used to the weather. No bugs and humidity."

Pope rubbed his fingers together. "It costs a pretty penny to inhabit this bug-less and humid-less world."

Pope and Dexter climbed a set of marble stairs and stood at the entrance of a twenty foot high oak door. Dexter rang the doorbell and heard a dog bark in the background. "How'd you get Maria to meet up with us? She wouldn't give me the time of day," Pope said.

"Call it country boy charm. You can't be pushy city boy. Watch and learn."

A woman with dark hair pulled up into a bun wearing Yoga pants and with a sculpted body to match opened the massive doors. She yelled over her shoulder, "Vladimir, stop hitting your sister... I'm sorry, it's been a long morning. My nanny isn't here today."

Dexter politely took off his John Deere hat and gave a sweet smile. He reached out a hand. "I'm sorry you're having a bad day. I have three kids of my own and they can drive a person crazy. We won't take long... just want to ask a few questions."

Maria gave Dexter a smile and then looked at Pope and gave him a scowl. "The only reason I'm doing this is because of his mother being sick. I've had a conversation with this one and I'm not in a chatty mood."

Dexter later explained to Pope that he'd used the sick mom card to get an interview with Maria.

Maria waved them into a foyer that flowed into a living space with massive windows that overlooked the beach. Two gold vases about six feet high sat on each side of the foyer and were accompanied by expensive art hanging on the walls. A sixty inch flat screen hung over a mantle and played cartoons. Two kids lay on the floor and were lost in TV Land, unaware of Dexter and Pope.

Maria leaned down to the boy stretched out on the fluffy white carpet. "I don't want to tell you again Vladimir. Stop hitting your sister or no Netflix the rest of the day."

The boy nodded. A young girl about seven stuck out her tongue at her brother. She glanced up at Dexter who was watching the scene unfold with amusement. "Who's that guy? His jeans are tight."

"Diane, that's rude. Don't say that. Just some friends who want to talk."

Dexter tipped his hat. "No problem ma'am. I'm used to getting strange looks in this town. My jeans are tight but not the skinny jean variety. These are Wrangler's, the country boy kind. Maybe that's what gave me away."

Maria wasn't amused with the jeans explanation. She ushered the men into the kitchen. A thirty by thirty island sat in the middle of the open space. Maria opened the fridge and pulled out a pitcher of Iced Tea. "You guys want something to drink?" she asked, pouring herself a glass.

The boys obliged. Maria found two glasses from a

cupboard. She poured the Iced Tea and asked if they wanted lemon. Both men nodded.

Maria took a swig of tea, placed the glass on the massive island, and pressed hard on the counter with her arms locking and veins bulging. "Things have been better since Boris left. Tired of those skanks coming around the house."

Dexter and Pope sipped their drinks and gave a look at one another. The details came out of nowhere. "Did you kick Boris out of the house?" Dexter asked.

"Hell, yeah. These girls were calling him on the phone, showing up at the house, and saying he was giving them a personal session in the home gym. I wasn't born yesterday," Maria said, taking another drink and staring out the windows.

Dexter asked, "How long ago did Boris leave?"

"When did he leave or when did I kick him out?"

"Either."

"Two weeks ago, give or take. I don't care. He's not welcome back in this home until some serious things change. He loves his work more than his family. And he loves every skank in that gym more than me," Maria said, wiping her eye. Her mascara ran on her cheek.

Dexter said, "I'm sorry. Can you tell me what happened the last time you saw him?"

Maria became animated and replayed the day like it was yesterday. "I came home from Hot Yoga. Went into the home gym and saw Boris with a skank. Told him to leave. Haven't seen him since."

"No calls or contact with Boris of any kind?"

"Nope. And don't care. He's probably staying with one of those girls. If that's what he wants, let him have it. I didn't move my entire life across the United States to be treated like leftovers."

Maria settled into a bar chair under the island. "Sorry for the drama. It's just been hard taking care of the kids and dealing with Boris' nonsense," she said, pausing, and then realizing she had another question, "Why are you here again? Is everything okay with Boris?"

Dexter glanced at Pope and then collected his thoughts. "Um, well, this is hard to say. Your husband's missing. And we think he's in trouble," Dexter said.

Maria seemed unphased by the news. "Not my problem."

"We think Boris might've kidnapped someone."

She rose from the bar stool. "Kidnapping? That doesn't sound like him. He's a moron and a cheater. But not a kidnapper. Are you sure?"

"No ma'am. That's why we wanted to talk with you today. We're still gathering information. If this is a kidnapping, we need to find him, and the victim."

"Who did he kidnap?"

"My dad," Pope blurted out.

"The guy who's partners with Roger Morris? He doesn't come around the gym much. Why would Boris kidnap your father?"

Pope shrugged. "Hard to tell. My dad went missing around the same time Boris was kicked out of your home. We think they're related."

"That could just be a coincidence," Maria said.

"You're right. And that's why we want to chase down every coincidence and see where it leads. Any reason Boris would have an issue with Mr. Pope?"

Maria tapped her long red finger nails on the granite countertop. She took a sip of her Iced Tea. "Not sure. He never talked about him. We barely saw him around the gym. None of this makes sense."

"Would your husband by chance be involved with gambling? Pope's father had some debts he hadn't paid before he went missing."

"Nothing out of the ordinary. Boris would place a few bets on the Laker's game or visit the horse track with his buddies. Just a bunch of guys having fun. No gambling problem."

"Do you have access to the finances? Check to see any abnormal withdrawals or deposits? Many guys with gambling debts are good at hiding it from their partners," Dexter said.

Maria shook her head. "I never worry about the finances. You see this place? As long as money was coming in and the bills were paid, if I could get groceries and take a yoga class, I never thought much about it. My husband's a lot of things, but he works hard, and takes care of his family. Could do without the cheating part..."

Dexter scribbled on his notepad and gave a weak smile. "I know this is hard for you ma'am. Only a few more questions and we'll be done."

Maria nodded.

"Would you have the names of anyone that might know his whereabouts? Any clients or friends that might've let him crash on the couch? You know, while you guys work things out? Everyone needs a comrade when things get hard in the home. I know this too well," Dexter said.

"I bet he's staying with this skank Molly, or Megan, some M name. She hangs around the gym and is always commenting on how great my husband looks. Her dad owned a place near Goldie's."

"Do you have an address?"

Maria opened a drawer under the island and wrote on a scrap piece of paper. "It's about a block from the gym. I think Boris was screwing her. Hard to say. Not the first, or the last."

Dexter looked at the paper and read the address. He smiled and reached out a hand. "Thank you for your time, Maria. We hope to track down your husband soon. All of your information is much appreciated. Have a good day and please contact us if you hear anything," Pope said, handing her a business card.

She gave Pope an annoyed glance.

Dexter and Pope let themselves out and jumped into the Honda. "What was going on in there? The awkwardness in that room you could cut with a knife," Dexter said, strapping on his seatbelt.

Pope wouldn't look Dexter in the eye. He nervously tapped his knees and played with the seatbelt in the Honda. "You like funny stories? Please don't share this with anyone. It's kind of embarrassing."

"Something weird was going on between you too. Did you say something to Maria to piss her off?"

"I wish. We slept together."

Dexter took off his John Deere hat and slapped Pope in the arm. "Come on... Is that why there was all this weird tension? How did that happen? You said your bed sheets were cold."

"When Dad went missing... I came to the house wanting to ask Maria questions. Her and Boris must've just got in a fight. Before I knew it we were rolling around in the sheets. It wasn't my most proud moment. Never mix work and pleasure."

"Damn, Pope. I thought you had no luck with the ladies?"

"I don't. Married lady in a crappy relationship has a fling with a Private Investigator in a moment of weakness. I shouldn't have been so judgmental with Mom. Maria hasn't talked to me since."

"That great, huh?"

"I'm what you call a one hit wonder."

"Did you sleep with the name Maria gave us? I need to know what we're working with."

"No, she's not my type. I only go for married and rich and vulnerable house wives," Pope said, firing up the Honda.

Pope scanned the address on the scrap of paper.

Dexter asked. "You know this girl?"

"It's Morris' daughter."

"This could get interesting," Dexter said, taking in one more glance at the Popov mansion, as the Honda sped away.

11

Dexter watched the streets of So Cal fly by, still in shock of the amount of people. The city walls were caving in with all their noise and speed. Pope leaned back in the Honda and drove with a face that said he needed sleep.

The visit with Maria was a good start in unraveling the case, but Dexter's heart longed for home. He wondered what Samantha was up to.

"You ever run into Morris' daughter?"

"I've met her a couple times."

"Where?"

"Why do you care?"

Pope's tone defensive and it threw Dexter off.

He raised his hands. "I'm not trying to be an ass. Just want all the facts. See where these leads take us. Remember, you liked my attention to detail. Everything okay?"

"Just tired. I've seen Morris' daughter at the gym. She lives next door to Goldie's. Morris owns a bunch of rental properties on the block."

"You a member at Goldie's?" Dexter asked.

"Is it a crime to want to stay in shape? Besides, I got a membership when they were running a special. I only pay $10 a month."

"Pops couldn't hook you up with a membership?" Dexter asked.

"He's not the generous type."

"That's too bad. But don't sell yourself short. You're a catch Pope... I see those abs. Strange the ladies don't come around more often? Wait, take that back. They do, they're just married."

"Ha, ha... I attract the vulnerable and broken. What does that say about me?" Pope said, with a yawn.

"Let's make this visit quick. You're in no shape for an all-nighter."

The sun set behind the horizon and the city street lights came to life. Dexter was amused with the glow of the city as it seemed so far from the slowness of LeClaire. A city with nothing resembling a downtown; unless you count the block of Main Street with its handful of eateries, a bank, coffee shop, thrift store, and other retail spaces.

Pope yawned again. "I'll be fine. Just need a pick me up. Let's stop at the Arco station. A Red Bull will get me back on track."

Pope left the Honda running and sprinted into the gas station. Dexter played with his phone and opened the Internet browser. He thought about Pope and Maria and the strange couple they'd make. The rich Russian woman and the single guy living in his sloppy apartment. Match made in heaven. Dexter typed in: Maria Popov.

The screen came back with a couple options. He clicked on the first name. Nope. A woman living in Russia selling children's literature. He scrolled down to the next link. He clicked.

A website populated his smartphone. It turned out Maria was an aspiring actress. Nothing big. Some commercials and a small role in Guys and Dolls at a local community theater. Dexter laughed at this crazy city. Everyone's an actress, actor, or aspiring to be one. The girl in the bar was right. If we call something a stereotype and it keeps coming true, maybe it's not.

Dexter checked out more of the website and nothing else seemed relevant. Pope opened the door of the Honda with a twenty ounce Red Bull. "Just what the doctor ordered. You miss me?"

Dexter held his phone in Pope's face. "Check this out. Mrs. Popov is an actress. Did you know?"

"I can't say our relationships lasted long enough to explore our aspirations and dreams. Boris likes the actresses for sure though."

"I've been here for a couple days and everyone I met wants to be famous. The girl in the bar. Maria. Boris isn't the only one with a thing for actresses."

"The odds of dating one in this town are high. It's not on purpose. I'm lucky to have anyone want to hang out with me. Actress, married lady, whoever."

"Maria better hope her acting career takes off. If her criminal husband goes to jail, she'll need cash. Unless she has access to some Russian mafia dollars. Which is always possible."

Five minutes later they arrived at Morris' daughter's apartment. It sat on Hampton Drive; a short walk to Goldie's. It was a two-story apartment and Jill lived on the top floor. The rent must've been high because of it being a prime location minutes from the beach. Dexter wondered how this young woman had money to afford such a place. Or how anyone did in this town! Roommates?

The bottom apartment was lit up. An older man sat smoking a cigarette and was oblivious to Dexter and Pope climbing the stairs. Dexter glanced through the window and noticed an unhealthy amount of pizza boxes.

Pope took the lead and made it to the top of the stairs. There was about a twenty foot landing leading to the front door. The porch light next to the screen door wasn't on. Pope unlocked his phone and directed a light on the door. A cat sleeping on the welcome mat leapt over the railing and scaled down the stairs to the bottom. Dexter grabbed his chest. "Damn cat scared me. Thought it was a coon."

"Coon?" Pope asked, flashing the light on Dexter.

"Raccoon."

Pope paused and caught his breath.

"Aren't you a gym rat? Ever hit the cardio machines?" Dexter asked.

"I hate cardio. More of a chest and arms guy. Ladies like it."

"Yeah, ladies love a guy with big arms, chicken legs, and someone who can't breathe after twenty stairs. Nothing like having a huge chest and dying of a heart attack."

Pope yawned. "You're not helping right now."

Pope gave a gentle knock on the screen door.

Nothing.

He peeled the white screen door back and noticed the front door was ajar. He glanced back at Dexter who was staring over the edge of the landing.

"The door's open," Pope said, flashing the phone light on the handle.

Pope and Dexter both drew their weapons. Pope nudged the door open and peered into the dark living room. A TV with the volume turned down glowed in the dark living room. Pope raised his pistol and scanned the open living room which flowed into a small dining area.

Dexter told Pope to check out the back of the apartment while he cleared the bedroom in the front. Dexter entered the front bedroom and noticed clothes and a mattress that was off its frame. Morris' daughter was a hoarder or liked to jump on the bed.

Dexter crawled over the piles of clothes and other random junk lining the floor. Picture frames covered a desk next to the bed. Dex leaned down and examined each one. Most of them were of different exotic locations. Each photo had a different guy. Jill Morris liked the men.

Pope yelled from the back of the apartment. Dexter rushed out of the bedroom to see what was happening. "I found something."

Jill Morris was naked and slumped in a pool of blood in the bathtub. It appeared she had taken her own life. Slash marks were on her wrists and the flickering of candles surrounded the edge of the tub.

Dexter knelt down next to the tub. "Her neck's bruised. That makes no sense."

"Why not?" Pope asked, with a sour look.

"If she slit her wrists why does she have bruising on her neck? Those are strangulation marks. Someone choked her out and then slashed her wrists. Ain't no suicide."

"I'm impressed country boy. You saw all of that that quick? Not bad for an amateur sleuth."

"Not my first rodeo, city slicker."

"Someone comes into the house, strangles Jill, slashes

her wrists... what about the candles? If someone kills themselves they wouldn't light candles, would they?"

Dexter yanked out his camera and shot a picture of the candles. He checked the quality of the picture and placed it back into his jean pocket.

"Why the photo?"

Dexter tilted his head. He examined the almost burnt-out candle on the left side of the tub. "See the wick... it's almost a nub. We can get a rough timeline from the wick. How long you guess a candle from Bath and Body would burn?"

"Bath and Body? How does a good ole boy know about B&B?"

Dexter smiled and glanced up at Pope who was standing in the bathroom's doorway trying to keep his dinner down. "You okay city slicker?"

Pope covered his mouth. "I don't like blood."

"Weakling. How long will that candle burn?"

"Don't know. Not a candle guy. Five hours? What's your take Sherlock Holmes?"

"Not a candle guy, either. But my wife once lit one in the bathroom after I took a dump. It was the size..."

"Please stop. I don't need to know the size of your turd."

"If you let me finish. The size of the candle at our house was like this one. We went to bed, and it was still burning in the morning. You sleep about 6-8 hours, right? I'm guessing by what's left of this wick the killer did this at least six hours ago."

Pope shook his head and couldn't believe what he heard. He knew Dexter was a competent detective despite not having any formal training. But this was beyond what he had expected bringing him to California. Dexter was a simple country guy with no education. He thought only law enforcement trained in big cities could handle big city crime. He was wrong. Dexter could hang with any city cop.

"Good work Missouri. I'll call the cops and let them finish up here," Pope said, fiddling with his phone.

Dexter left the bathroom and needed some new scenery. The sight of a beautiful young girl sitting in her own blood was working his stomach over. Not because he didn't like blood. Too close to home. He thought of his daughters and Samantha. Couldn't imagine losing any of them. Pope followed Dexter out to the front of the apartment in the living room.

Dexter stepped into the front bedroom again and called Pope to take a peek inside. Pope finished with the phone call and shoved the phone back inside his pocket. "What man? I'm tired and want to leave as soon as the cops arrive."

Dexter stood akimbo inside the bedroom. Pope commented on the mess of the room and wondered what the killer wanted with Jill. "I think Jill was getting around in Venice."

"Why's that?"

"Check out these photos. Every one is of a different guy in an exotic location. Beaches, mountains, safaris, and Europe. The apartment doesn't scream of someone with money. Yet Jill can swing trips around the world? These dudes must have dough."

"Everyone has a story. Let's honor her death and not pry into her personal life. She's gone, and we got what we need."

"For a private eye you sure don't seem interested in these possible leads. One of these guys might be the killer. Should we take a picture of the frames?"

Pope appeared agitated and didn't want to look at the pictures. He stroked his hair and ignored the comment. "I think we're good. Jill isn't important. We need to find my dad and Boris."

Dexter noticed a frame on a dresser across the bedroom. He hadn't seen it the first time. He walked over and glanced at the photo. "I've always wanted to go to the beach. California's my first visit to a real body of water. Lake LeClaire doesn't count. It's manmade and stocked with fish."

Pope stood in the doorway and watched for the cops to arrive. He was antsy and looking to leave. "We'll go in the water tomorrow. Can we leave now? I think I hear the cops downstairs."

"Sure thing," Dexter said, holding up the frame, "Jill looked so happy in this picture. The beach is beautiful. But something is off. I've seen this dude."

Pope ignored the comment.

Dexter held the frame in Pope's face, "I know you said you have a familiar face. Well, this guy must be your twin."

Pope turned away from the photo. "Okay, you caught me. Jill and I were an item. I didn't kill Jill if that's what you're thinking."

Dexter placed the frame back on the dresser and raised his hands. "No one's accusing you of anything. You seem a little nervous. I'm just trying to gather information to solve a case and you keep lying... lover boy."

"Screw you, Dexter. I'm no killer. Jill and I dated for a minute and had some fun. It was a long time ago."

"For a guy who claims not to be good with the ladies, you'd make a lot of single dudes jealous. Maria, Jill, the girl from the bar. Another notch in your belt. Anything else you're hiding?"

Pope rubbed his eyes.

"The cops are here."

"How are you going to explain the picture of you and the dead girl? Not a good look, Pope."

Pope hung his head. "I'm tired and can't think straight. I didn't kill that girl...."

Dexter lifted the frame from the dresser and jammed it under his shirt in the back of his jeans. "A get out of jail free card. I'm doing this one as a favor. But you have some explaining to do."

12

The cops questioned Pope for a few minutes. He made up a story about checking on Jill for her father. Pope and Dexter returned to the apartment and went straight to bed with minimal talking.

The next day Pope had visited his office for paperwork and to follow up with a few clients. Another stalking situation for an unsuspecting first date. Business was drying up because all his attention was being hijacked trying to find his father and Boris. Stalking first dates paid okay, but wasn't sustainable in the long run.

Dexter lounged on a striped couch that scratched his skin as he moved around. "Where'd you get the couch? It's making my skin turn red."

"Found it on the curb. Cleaned it up. Money gets tight when you run your own business. You can relate, running that junk collecting biz."

"Amen, brother. And it's not junk, we call it rusty gold. I called John this morning to see how Antique Adventures was doing. He said they closed the store early yesterday because he needed a mental health day. What a moron.

That's money down the tubes. It's hard to not want to do everything yourself."

Pope nodded and tapped on a laptop. He was checking email and not all that interested in the conversation. Dexter strolled over to a table in the corner of the office. He placed his gun on the table and then emptied the chamber. He stared into the holes where the bullets used to be. "Can we talk about the giant elephant in the room?"

Pope tapped at the keys and gave a half smile. "My friend was also throwing away that elephant too," he said, glancing to a ceramic elephant piggy bank propped on a bookshelf.

"Don't dodge the question. Why was there a picture of you in Jill's house?"

"I told you, Dex. We dated for a few months. Nothing serious, and we moved on. The story of my life. Don't worry about it."

"I'm not worried. My trip to California is playing with house money. You paid my way. I'm here to help you. But I need you to be honest. What's the scoop on Jill? And whatever else is going on? Time to come clean..."

"Nope. Just a fling, end of story," Pope said, leaning in closer to read the thirteen inch screen on his laptop.

Dexter reinserted the bullets into his gun. He playfully pointed it at Pope, who was oblivious to Dexter. "I will use this thing if you're not telling the truth," he said, squinting one eye, and pretending to aim it at Pope's head.

Dexter stood next to the desk where Pope was still lost in a sea of emails. "Can you look at my eyes?" Dexter said, sitting on the edge of the desk. "The only thing keeping me here is your mother. I want to help you solve this case. But if I'm being lied to... I'm done. Home life's a mess. Flying back to Missouri is the adult thing to do. But, I'm a man-child... and will stay as long as it takes. Be honest Pope."

Pope slid back into his swivel chair and put his hands behind his head. "Okay, you caught me. I told you that my love life was a mess. Maria and Jill don't jive with my story. I get it. But these chicks don't love me. They were flings. I'm embarrassed to even call these relationships. And now one of them is dead," Pope said, swiping a tear from his cheek.

"Damn. Did you love Jill?" Dexter asked.

"No way. I'm just raw right now. My mom, dad, and this shitty business; it's a lot. I had it so good at LAPD, the dream job. And I screwed it up. I let my anger get the best of me... and the drugs. No serious leads on a relationship. What am I doing with my life?"

"Free tip. Don't call women 'leads.' Kind of sucks all the romance out. You'll find someone man. You're a good looking dude who knows his way around a crime scene and the gym. That must mean something, right? Women are still a mystery. My relationship is on life support and the first marriage ended in death. We're not much different. Life gives you lemons, make lemonade, or some shit."

Pope liked Dexter's pep talk. Something about commiserating with the pain of others brings comfort. "Good to know you're as dysfunctional as me. They say you're the product of the five people you hang around. You're rubbing off."

"I'm not taking all the credit," Dexter said, holstering his gun.

Dexter gave Pope a fist bump and strolled back to the itchy couch. He slumped into the cushions and reached for a magazine on the coffee table. "But there's one thing that's driving me crazy. I've been thinking about it since last night. Isn't it odd that all the women you sleep with are actresses? Maria, the girl at the bar."

"Like I said. It's not weird when you live in La La Land.

Everyone moves here to find fame. Most don't. It's what we're known for," Pope said, reengaging with his email.

"True. But here's another weird coincidence," Dexter said, holding up a Play Bill from a local theater company. "Strange that Jill Morris would be on the cover of the Long Beach Play House. Maria... the chick at the bar... And Jill? That makes three. Some say trouble comes in threes. Is this a fetish or something?"

"Drop it, please. Not sure of the relevance?"

Dexter rose from the couch and pulled his pistol from his jeans. He aimed it at Pope's head. "The moment I landed in California something didn't feel right. It wasn't the sushi or the amount of grown men with man-buns. Something off in my gut. And now I know. It's you, Pope. Your acting chops aren't bad. The helpless single guy. A failing business and sick mother. But I'm not sure how convincing you are. Isn't it strange Boris attracts only actresses to his gym? Isn't it strange that you only attract actresses into your bed? I want to believe you Pope, but my bullshit radar is blinking fast."

Pope surrendered and stood up from the swivel chair. He gave a nervous smile. "Dexter, you have no idea what you're talking about. You think I'd lie about Mom's cancer, the business? Bills stacked so high I can't sleep most nights? A dad who's an asshole and treated me like trash as a kid? This is no act. Someone taught me to take responsibility and not make excuses. And this is what I needed to do," Pope said, yanking a pistol from his desk drawer, and aiming it at Dexter.

Dexter held steady and sweat was beading up on his forehead. He rubbed the side of his pistol with his thumb. "Don't do anything stupid, Jake. Come clean and we forget this ever happened. Water under the bridge."

"Stop the shit, country boy. You pretend to be a cop but

you would never hack it in a real city. All your bullshit petty crime in LeClaire. The time I spent in Missouri was a joke."

"If I recall you got shot and almost died. Not so petty... Can we talk about jokes? Who gets sent to small town USA if they're such a good cop in the big city, as you say? I've seen more darkness in LeClaire to last a lifetime. I wouldn't be concerned with having a pissing contest right now. You're the one caught with your pants down. So while we're chatting. Did you kill Jill?"

"Ha... Jill was a whore and deserved what came to her. She dated every dude in Venice. I wouldn't waste a good bullet on that skank."

"You want to explain your fascination with the actresses? You and Boris working together?"

"That Russian idiot? Boris caught lightening in a bottle at Goldie's. Had his fifteen minutes of fame. These whores signing up for personal training because he promised them roles in his movies."

"His movies? What movies?"

"Pornography. Boris was shooting low budget movies at his house and other places in the city. You think he made all his money on gym memberships and personal training? No one's owning a mansion in Manhattan Beach on PT cash."

"Were you planning on telling me all this stuff about Boris?"

"I've been watching him since he moved to LA. Thought I could get in on the action."

"Please no, Pope. Tell me you're not doing porno movies?"

"Hell no. I'm just doing favors for Boris and his crew. I need the money."

"So you bring me out to California and it turns out you're drinking vodka with the Russians. Ain't that something..." Dexter said, shaking his head, while still holding the gun steady on Pope. "I should end you right now."

"You won't. I knew you weren't the sharpest pencil in the box. Like taking candy from a baby."

"Funny... if I'm so dull how'd I figure out you're banging Jill, and Maria? Why did you waste your time and money bringing me out here? I got better things to do."

Pope crept in close to Dexter with the gun aimed at his neck. "You're the outsider we've been looking for. Someone no one would expect anything from. We got a job for you."

"We... who's we?"

"It doesn't matter. My team and I are excited at what you bring to the table."

"You are a world of contradictions. I thought I was a dull pencil. You run a PI business out of a rat infested apartment. What kind of team you talking about?" Dexter said, stepping back as Pope came in close.

"You might be familiar with the country lyric: I got friends in low places. Well, I have friends in high places. There's a lot of things you don't know about me, Dexter."

"I know you're a liar and have anger issues. The reason you were shipped off to LeClaire. I know you almost died after a crazy racist cult leader tried to take you and Detective Stearns out. And I was the one who saved your ass and made sure you were okay after surgery. My friends may be from the low country where the whiskey's dry... but at least they're loyal."

"Loyalty's overrated. And besides, aren't we all a little angry, Dexter? I've seen the rage inside you. Isn't that why you hate seeing the bad guys win? Isn't that why your wife is always five minutes away from leaving you?"

"Don't bring my family into this. I ain't no Pharisee. At

least I'm honest about my shit. Tell me who you're working with? This team..."

Pope trained the gun on Dexter and walked back near the laptop on the desk. He reached down to a black duffel bag slumped next to the desk. "I want to make your trip worthwhile. You scratch my back, and I scratch yours. A little birdie told me Antique Adventures ain't doing so good. After you opened that second store you're bleeding money," Pope said, spilling out piles of cash onto the ground.

"For a guy who's supposed to be broke that's a lot of scratch. Money talks. Who told you about the store?"

"It doesn't matter. You want in?"

"What's the job?"

"I have some young ladies doing work in the movie industry. We'd like to see them become stars. And you're going to help."

Dexter glanced at the money and back at Pope. "I ain't running no porno business if that's what you're alluding to. Count me out. I'd rather go home and call it a day."

Pope nodded to the corner of the office near the front door. It slammed open and a large man grabbing the arms of a larger man waltzed into the space. "Good news, you don't have to work alone. We brought you some help. Your partner in crime. Do what we say and you live. Let's not even consider the alternative."

John Wood, Dexter's best friend, and partner at Antique Adventures, stood in the middle of the room with his arms tied and mouth gagged. He was sweaty as usual.

Who was watching the store?

13

T he Odessa Film Studio was about twenty minutes from Venice Beach. A bleak and plain looking warehouse, with a logo of a TV camera centered above the entrance. Dexter, John, and Pope pulled up to a security shack leading to the back lot of the studio. Pope gave a thumbs up and a Russian man with a crew cut raised the security arm attached to the shack.

Dexter and John glanced out of the window like tourists from another planet. John commented on how busy LAX was and how he'd never seen so many cars and people. Dexter concurred and wondered why anyone travels anywhere.

Pope parked the Honda in the back lot. They entered a backdoor into the studio. Sliding doors dumped them into what appeared to be a movie set. "You boys ever been on a real Hollywood set?" Pope asked, with a grin.

John glanced at Dexter and scratched his head. "Do you know who you're dealing with? These country boys don't leave LeClaire all that much. So we'll go with no..."

"This is where the magic happens."

Dexter scanned the set and watched girls running in and out of a makeshift living room. A man called cut, and a bell rang in the distance. "What's with the news set? That looks like WB-4 in Missouri. Is this a news station?"

"Something like that..." Pope said and bolted toward a man sitting in a director's chair.

John found a long table covered in chips, sodas, bagels, and other snacks. He swiped a bagel and Diet Coke. "It's not Cherry Coke, but it will have to do."

Dexter smacked him in the head. "Stop messing around. We have to take this seriously. I don't want to go home in a body bag. And finding one in your size will be difficult, chubby. Put down the bagel..."

"I'm a stress eater."

"Who's watching the store?"

"Samantha."

"Shit, you're joking right? What did you tell her?"

"Told her I'd be gone a few days. Some big Russian came into the store and pretended to know you. He said he wanted to fly me to California. He said it was to help with the case."

"You moron. Some Russian guy you don't know wants to fly you to California and you ask no questions?"

"He sounded legit. Besides, my mental health isn't good right now. I needed some John time. And I wanted to help you, Dex."

"You shut down the store for personal reasons? Well, now you're helping... helping us get killed. Samantha ask about me?"

"She was working on some end of the year stuff. Samantha didn't say much. You guys still on the rocks?"

"Yep. And this little adventure isn't helping. I guess if I

die she can find a new husband. She might be wishing that upon me as we speak."

"Stop talking like that. We'll find a way out of this mess. We always do. I can tell you're stressed. Eat a donut," John said, handing Dexter a powdered donut from the craft services table.

Dexter knocked the donut on the floor as Pope came up to the table. "I see you found craft services. Please help yourself to anything you like. It's for our actors and the crew. What's mine is yours," Pope said, sipping on a coffee.

Dexter watched Pope eat a bagel and seethed with anger. He wanted to rip out his pistol and put a bullet in Pope's face. He couldn't believe how betrayed he felt. One moment Pope is bemoaning his lack of relationships and money. Now it appears he's working for a shady Russian operation and living on easy street. Doing God knows what in their low budget studio. Dexter wondered if the story about his mother was true.

Dexter probed further. "What's going on here? Everything out of your mouth is a lie these days. Is the story of your mom true? Does she have cancer, and is she even your mother?"

Pope munched on the bagel and gulped a coffee. "Come on, Dex. You were in that horrible room. What do you think she's an actress? Or is she...?"

"Is she?"

"No way man. My mom is sick as hell."

"Doesn't look like you're having trouble paying the bills. You running the studio?" Dexter said, staring at the lights hanging from the rafters.

"Kind of, it's complicated. Not important right now. We need to give you country boys the grand tour. Get a feel for the work you'll be doing. Before long, you'll want to live in the big city and rake in some serious Hollywood dollars."

John inhaled another donut and thought of Hollywood dollars. He dreamed of swimming in a vault of money and beautiful woman in bikinis feeding him chips and Diet Cherry Coke. John needed some Hollywood money so he could move out of his mom's basement.

"Keep your tainted dollars. I'm only here for my kids," Dexter blurted out.

"I thought you were here for my mother? Your tune has changed," Pope said.

"If your mother has cancer, and is your *real* mom, fine. I wish her the best. But my motivation has changed. I do what you say, finish the job, you keep your promise... and we're out. Back to LeClaire. I'm doing this to get back to my kids."

A man in a ponytail and jeans carrying a clipboard came up to John and Dexter at the craft services table. "Hey, fellas. My name is Vladimir. Glad you'll be joining the team."

He held out his hand and Dexter ignored the gesture. "Not a team I'd like to play on."

The man gave a confused look and glanced at John. "See you've found the craft services table. Please help yourself, what's ours is yours. You want to meet some of the girls you'll be working with?"

John chomped on a glazed donut and with a mouth full of sugary dough tried to talk, "Hell, yeah. Are these Russians mail-order brides?"

Dexter slugged him in the shoulder.

The pony-tailed man laughed and glanced at his clipboard. "No, sir. Most are So Cal girls. Not a huge Russian population in La La Land. At least not yet."

John nodded. "Are they single? I'm looking for the future Mrs. Wood."

Dexter couldn't believe John's comments despite the weight of the situation. John had been single most of his life. Mostly because he lived with his mom, had an unhealthy obsession with video games, and didn't get out much. Other than that he was a catch. He'd tried online dating with little success as LeClaire is not a hotbed for singles. Most people get married to their high school sweethearts or move away to find life outside the suffocating existence of small town living. Dexter knew LeClaire could suffocate, but sometimes familiar air is the best kind to breathe.

The pony-tailed man said, "We have a little bit of everything. Single girls. Married moms trying to make a name for themselves. And girls engaged to another actor on set. But let's not get sidetracked with your primary mission. Recruitment. With all the films we're making, finding quality actors is not an easy task. That's why we have you guys."

"Yeah, baby. I'm all about hunting down girls," John said, wiping the flakes of glazed donut off the corner of his mouth.

"Please ignore my chubby friend. Recruitment? That's not what I understood to be the mission. I thought we were trying to find Boris. I'm not recruiting girls for whatever weird films you're shooting," Dexter said, staring off to the movie set.

The tone of Vladimir changed. His happy expression turned to that of someone akin to eating a sour lemon. He moved in close to Dexter and tapped his chest. Dexter recoiled.

"Listen country boys. You belong to us now. You do what we say or things go sideways real quick. Not only will things go bad for you and your fat friend, but anyone related to you. Russian power runs very, very, deep. Got it?"

Dexter wasn't often scared, but the ice in the room went

through his body. The honesty of Vladimir's threat made Dexter uneasy. He thought of Samantha and his kids being in harm's way. Nothing would stir up a hornet's nest inside Dexter like Samantha getting hurt.

Dexter held up his hands and backed away from the warm breath of the Russian. "Easy... I get it. Tell us what to do."

John and Dexter followed the Russian to a back dressing room. Dozens of women young and old were practicing lines in the mirror, adjusting their costumes and hair, and applying makeup in a long line of mirrors.

"This better not be no porn studio. You aren't making snuff films are you?" Dexter asked.

The Russian tapped on his clipboard. "No, country boy. I would never subject our women to that filth. Our studio has a reputation to keep. And has a different agenda. A message of hope for the world."

Dexter pointed to the news set. "Is that what the news desk is all about?"

"You're very perceptive, Mr. O'Kane. Yes, we're sending our message around the world with our talented actors."

"What message is that? Communism? Power? Hate?"

The Russian gave a cough like something was caught in his throat. "I'll explain later. What's important right now is you and your chubby friend find more beautiful people to share our story with the world."

A petite blonde girl came from behind the sea of actors prepping themselves for whatever films they were shooting. She appeared shy, and hesitated to extend a hand. The Russian ushered her in front of the guys "This is Lilly Thompson. One of our up-and-coming actors. Say hello."

"Hello," Lilly said, pushing a sliver of her blonde locks around her ear.

Dexter sensed she wasn't thrilled with the studio and appeared uncomfortable in her own skin. "Hey, Lilly. Any big parts these days?"

She glanced at the Russian and back at Dexter. "I'm not supposed to tell. Our acting coaches say it's bad luck when you talk about your art before you share it."

John and Dexter nodded, not sure what she meant. "How'd you get involved with acting?" Dexter asked.

"I did some plays in High School and some local community theater. Being an actress like Meryl Streep has always been my dream."

Dexter nodded, having no clue who Meryl Streep was. "Where'd you go to school?"

"Venice High. Born and raised in the area."

"College? Did you try getting into acting school?" John asked.

Lily swayed side to side and stared at the floor. She appeared uncomfortable with the question. "UCLA for a minute. It didn't work out."

"What happened?" Dexter asked.

"I met a guy. He told me UCLA was a waste of time."

Vladimir cut her off. "Ok, Lilly. Thank you for coming over and meeting the guys. We have work to do. You can leave now."

Without hesitation Lily stomped off and disappeared into the hordes of women prepping and primping and coloring their faces. John sipped on a Diet Coke. "That got weird in a hurry. What dude crushed her dreams?"

Vladimir flipped a page on his clipboard. "Lilly doesn't always tell the truth. Well, boys, it's time for the next item on the agenda. Looks like we have to discuss the recruiting process. Jake Pope will be your trainer."

"Does he have to be? He's not on my Christmas card list right now," Dexter said.

"Sorry Mr. Dexter. You have no say. Jake is one of our best men. He'll take good care of you."

"Whatever."

"Good, glad we're on the same page. I'll call an Uber and we'll get you to the Odessa. Rest up. Tomorrow will be a full day. Our message's reach depends on your ability to recruit. So don't mess this up."

Dexter and John hopped in the Uber, a black minivan, and headed to a hotel a couple miles away. The rage inside Dexter was brewing, and this had to an end sooner than later.

John fell asleep in the car.

14

John and Dexter settled into the Odessa Hotel off Juniper and Sunset. It was a modern place with a sleek and sterile design. They found their room on the second floor and turned on ESPN. Maybe something familiar would ease their minds from the crazy world they found themselves in.

John propped up a pillow on a queen bed and crawled into the comfortable sheets. "Damn, Dex. The softness of the sheets. The mattress has some kind of pillow on top. It's like lying on clouds. Nothing like my bed at home."

"You still sleeping with those Star Wars sheets?"

"Those are sentimental. Sum up my childhood"

"When Star Wars came out. Last time you had a date?"

John threw a pillow to the other queen bed Dexter had now been resting on. It hit him in the head.

"Stop messing around chubby. We need to focus. I'll be damned if we spend our first trip to the coast under the thumb of some dumbass Russians."

John smiled and flipped through the channels on the fifty-inch flat screen.

"Why are you smiling?" Dexter asked.

"You're not invincible, Dex."

"Who said I was?"

"I saved you this time. Remember that."

"Saved me? How did you save me? The Russians kidnapped you from LeClaire, tied you up, and flew you to California. Now we're working for the Russian mob. Please explain yourself."

"I'm so right. It's like the good Lord knew without my help there would be no chance in hell you'd get out of here alive. Now I'm here. I saved you..."

"We're not saved, yet. You have too much Diet Cherry Coke on the brain. Come back to earth. We need a plan to get home."

John eased into the five pillows propping up his chunky head and his eyes started getting heavy. He flipped the channels and dozed off. John never found ESPN.

Every channel looked unfamiliar. Not your normal cable package. Someone translated the stations into Russian and the actors and newscasters were all women. The studio from earlier in the day buzzed through Dexter's mind. He could picture all the women in those dressing rooms on the TV despite not recognizing any one individual.

Dexter tossed a pillow at John, who was about to fall asleep. "Wake up! You notice anything on the TV?"

"That ain't no English. And they're *all* girls."

"Good work, Sleepy. Why don't you try to stay awake for over five minutes so we can figure some stuff out?"

"If I don't get twelve hours a sleep at night, I'm no good to anyone. Last night was rough."

"Another reason you live with your mother. And why you never show up to Antique Adventures before ten. Does moms let you sleep that much?"

"Oh, yeah. She encourages it. Says I was a premature baby and I'm still catching up on sleep."

"You've obviously grown out of your small frame, chubby," Dexter said, with a thumbs up, "What do you think the Russians are trying to do? What's the message they keep blabbering about?"

"With all the ladies, it doesn't appear to be a message of violence. Not that women can't be nasty. I've seen plenty of ladies at O'Malley's want to rip your face off if you stare at them wrong. But they are nothing like what we dealt with last year and those American Renaissance nut jobs."

Dexter laughed. "True. Jarrett Stevens was a monster. And Pope isn't the dude we worked with in LeClaire. He's got some demons inside. Been lying to me since I arrived here in So Cal. I don't trust him as far as I can throw him."

A clicking sound came from the corner of the room. Then grinding. "You hear that?" John asked.

"What noise? It's probably the Coke in your belly sloshing around."

"No. It was like a grinding noise. Like gears turning."

John rose from the bed and heard it again. He glanced up to the ceiling and spotted a camera mounted in the corner. It had a red eye like a snake. He stood under the eye of the camera. "Found it," John said, placing a finger on his lips.

John whispered, "I think they're watching us. Probably listening too."

John farted. "They can enjoy a John Special with extra beef."

Dexter rose from the bed, plugged his nose, and stared up at the camera. He waved his hands side to side and watched the camera move in spastic motion. They thought it was funny. "I don't give a shit if they hear us, see us, or smell us," Dexter shook his head at John, "They can come and get us. We're going home in once piece."

"Please don't get us killed, yet. I have good years left on the tires. If we're going to die, I want it on our own terms."

Dexter back peddled to the bed and plopped on the edge. He placed his head in his hands. "I'm sorry, bro. I never saw things going this way. I'm tired and miss my family. Wanna go home."

"That lady on TV selling jewelry says: home is where the heart is. But I'd keep your heart somewhere else for now," John said.

"Why's that?" Dexter asked, scratching the side of his unshaven face.

"Before the Russians kidnapped me. Samantha was at the shop. She's still pissed at you. Said something about fences never being mended. She was even more pissed knowing I was coming to California to visit."

"I thought she was clueless? Does Samantha think I'm in trouble?"

"No. The Russians made it seem we were friends. I think she's in the dark. But the fence thing sounds serious."

Dexter rose from the bed and paced the room. The camera grinded in the background. "Damn, I always hated fixing the fence at the house. Let alone the fence of our relationship. The fence on the house is a lot easier to mend."

Dexter realized he was being loud and used a lower voice in case the camera had audio. "Samantha and the kids are the only family I got. And you. I keep screwing things up. If I lose you guys, I lose everything. And here I am, same story, different characters. Russian communists."

"Technically Russians aren't Communist. They're a quasi-form of democracy. It's been that way since 1991. Pick up a history book. It would be good for ya."

"Thank you professor. Then what's their message? Communism is dead. What virus they trying to spread?" Dexter said, standing to the right of the TV.

"Since Putin has been in office, it's all power politics. Show the world you have the biggest balls. I don't know about all them rumors of the Russians interfering with the election. But it's about world domination and money. Power and money is what this country runs on. Putin seems like a psycho. I hope whatever propaganda these folks are peddling it ain't tied to him."

Dexter reached for the remote. He turned up the volume. "These girls are so young. Look at their faces. It's like they're brainwashed. Puppets in a Russian cult."

"Turn it off. I don't like watching this stuff. I wish we could see the score of the Chiefs game."

Dexter turned off the TV and tossed the remote on the bed. He leaned against a window that overlooked a street below. Thousands of cars blew by. He glanced at the camera and back out the window. "This is a crazy place. I don't know what the next move is... But we'll know when to act. We always do..."

"Hope so. I'm getting hungry. Are we allowed to leave the hotel and get some grub?" John said, rubbing his inflated stomach.

The phone on the night stand rang. Dexter glanced at John who was reading a room service menu. "Hello, this is Dexter."

"Mr. O'Kane. We are sending up an evening chaperone. She will show you around and make sure you're taken care of. Her name is Lilly," the man said, with a Russian accent, hanging up the phone in abrupt fashion.

"Was that Putin?"

"Funny... They're sending a chaperone. Name's Lilly."

"Like the girl we met at the studio."

Dexter shrugged his shoulders. "I don't like the sound of a chaperone. We don't need no babysitter."

"Have an open mind. Maybe they just want to show us Disneyland. I love Mickey Mouse."

Dexter ignored the comment.

There was a knock on the door. John answered the door and a young girl danced into the room. "Hey, fellas. I guess I'm your date tonight."

"Date?" John asked.

"Not like a real date. It's just a joke we have with the other girls. I'm your chaperone for the night. Can I show you around? You guys hungry?"

"How'd you know?" John said, rubbing his stomach.

"We have our ways," Lilly said, batting her eyelashes.

"You the girl we saw earlier at the studio?"

"Yep."

"I thought you were an actress? Why are you our chaperone tonight? Aren't there some mean Russian mobsters to make sure we don't run away?" Dexter said, with a hint of sarcasm.

"No way, Mr. O'Kane. Our organization is not violent. We're here to promote the most important message in the world and display our talents."

Dexter paused, as he was intrigued by the robotic like quality Lilly's voice took on. Here face reminded him of the girls on the TV. It was like she was reading off a teleprompter and something inside her had died. Her words felt ingenuous.

"What is your message... if you don't mind me asking?" Dexter said.

Lilly ignored the comment. "It's not important right now.

What's important is getting you boys some authentic California food in your bellies. You up for Mexican?"

Dexter and John gave a thumbs up.

Lilly smiled. "Great! I know a great place nearby."

Lilly and the boys piled into a green Toyota Prius. John commented about the size. It was like trying to cram clowns into a car at the circus. John ended up in the backseat and was not happy about it.

Dexter stared out of the window of the car. The images of the women filled his mind.

15

Lilly raced through the streets of LA with Dexter and John crammed in the Prius. She tapped on the steering wheel as a Taylor Swift song echoed through XM Radio.

"What is this junk?" John asked, from the backseat.

"You're not referring to one of the great pop stars of our time. This is Taylor Swift. You Belong with Me."

"I don't belong to nobody. Is this country? I can't stand it," John said.

"What's wrong with it?" Lilly asked, in a sweet tone.

Dexter shook his head listening to Lilly and John argue. "Country these days sounds like Bubble Gum music from the 50s. It has no heart. What happened to the gritty stuff like Johnny Cash and Merle Haggard? Those guys were tough as nails."

"What are you, a country music aficionado? Give me some more artists."

"Where to begin? Willie Nelson, Patsy Cline, John Dexter. This little girl ain't country. She's talking about stuff she knows little about. I'm guessing she grew up in a wealthy suburb. She ain't never shot a gun or saddled a horse."

"How do you know?" Lilly asked.

"You hear it in her voice. This girl is soft."

Lilly waved off Dexter and bopped her head to the music. "Whatever... Taylor Swift is a genius. She doesn't do *just* country. She can sing anything. That's why she's so great."

"Great artists have their own style. They don't need to change with the tides of culture. They play from the gut. These bubble gum songs aren't from a deep place, they're shallow. Fifty years from now everyone will forget this junk. The cream always rises to the top."

Lilly pulled the Prius into a parking spot at Casa Sanchez off Broadway and Paramount Blvd. The building was run down, which was a good sign for great Mexican food in LA. "I'll pretend this conversation never happened. You watch, we will sing Taylor Swift for generations. Not that you old guys will be around," Lilly said, with a wink.

"Old guy jokes. I see how it is. Let's eat, we're starving," John said, licking his lips.

Lilly and the boys walked up to the counter inside the restaurant and ordered their food. Tacos, lots of tacos. They filled up their sodas and chatted at their table while waiting for someone to call their numbers.

John sipped on a Cherry Coke. "How'd you get into the acting business?"

Lilly's face lit up. "My mom was a B-List actress in Hollywood in the 70s and 80s. Being on sets as a kid did something inside me. I thought the actors were superheroes. I guess it was something I'd always wanted to do."

"Family business, huh?" Dexter asked.

"Something like that. I watched my mom struggle to find

parts. She did some commercials and small roles in movies and TV. But she loved it. She said never stop dreaming and good things would happen. I guess that stuck with me. I can't say I've had much success so far. But I'm working hard and not giving up the dream."

Dexter nodded. "Have you played in anything we'd have seen?"

Lilly stared at the floor and played with her straw. She stumbled over her sentences. "Not, yet. My time will come. Boris says I have talent. He says I'll be a household name someday."

"Boris? Who's Boris?"

"Boris Popov."

Dexter and John traded glances. "You know Boris? How did you meet?"

"At the gym. He was my trainer. Most of the girls at Odessa have met Boris. He says I will be a star," Lilly said, monotone.

"Would you know where Boris is?"

Lilly thought. "Funny, come to think of it, I haven't seen him in a few weeks. I injured my calf and haven't been to the gym. Boris doesn't come around the studio that often anymore. He's a busy guy. Trying to spread our message is a full-time job."

"Isn't Boris a personal trainer? How does he have time to spread this message you talk about?" Dexter asked.

Lilly shrugged. "He just does it. Ask any of the ladies. They all love Boris."

A worker in the restaurant called their numbers and John got the food. He passed out the tacos and burritos to everyone. A basket of chips and salsa sat in the middle of the table. John dragged a chip into the bowl and piled on some salsa. He bit into the chip and sighed. "So good!"

Dexter ignored the comment and tried to reengage with Lilly. "You said the ladies love Boris? What did you mean?"

Lilly wiped her mouth of a glob of guacamole from her burrito. A smile grew on her face. "Boris has many suitors. But he said I will be a star. We have a special relationship."

"Isn't he married to Maria?"

Lilly slapped her burrito remnants into a red basket covered in paper. "Please don't say her name. She doesn't know how good she has it. Boris is kind, thoughtful, and the most loving man. If she treated him half as good as I do. I'd hardly call it a marriage. It's pretty much over. We'll probably move in together soon."

"Are you and Boris sleeping together?"

"I don't talk about my love life," Lilly said, taking a bite on a chip, and washing it down with soda. "Girls don't kiss and tell."

"I'm sorry for being nosy. But the more information you can give me the better. Boris is missing and our job is to bring him back." Dexter said.

"What? Didn't know, I'm a nobody in the organization. Is he okay?" Lilly said, panicking.

"We have no idea. Can you tell us the last time you saw him?" John asked, now leaning back enjoying a full belly.

She tapped her nails on the wooden table top. Lilly thought for a second and scrunched her mouth to the side. "We saw him at the studio a couple weeks back. Boris came into my dressing room and was acting weird. He was stressing about something. Boris had to travel and wouldn't be around. I thought nothing of it. He travels all the time spreading our message."

"Did he say anything else?" John asked.

Lilly sipped on her drink and placed it on the table. A

tear was building in the corner of her eye. "He wasn't sure our relationship would make it."

"So you were an item?" Dexter asked.

"He was my soulmate. I'm still hoping. He said when he got back from his trip we could talk more. This isn't the first time."

"What happened before?"

"He has a reputation. Sometimes he's not faithful. But he always comes back. I caught him with another girl. It's the price you have to pay with a genius."

"Why is Boris a genius? He sounds like a lying douche bag. If Boris is a genius, I'm Einstein," John blurted out.

"He knows the talent. Boris built an empire almost overnight. Many girls have gone on to TV and movies. They became stars. He promised I'd be a star. Geniuses can't be tied down. That's what he tells me."

"Geniuses can be crazy, too. I'm not sure what Kool Aid y'all are drinking, but Boris sounds like a bad dude," Dexter said finishing his tacos.

"Why do you care then?" Lilly asked with a stern look.

"I don't. It's kind of the situation we found ourselves in. Jake Pope's a liar, and here we are."

Lilly picked at her food. Wouldn't look at the boys. She picked at her food.

"You're not banging Jake are you?" Dexter asked.

Lilly hesitated...

The front door of Casa Sanchez burst open and two men in black suits rushed in and grabbed Lilly. One other wide shouldered man in dark glasses watched the door. The workers of the restaurant cursed in Spanish from behind the counter.

Dexter and John held up their hands.

They dragged away Lilly without a word.

One man hesitated at the entrance and tossed a set of keys to Dexter, "Take the car back to the hotel. Wait for our instructions. If you do not listen to our orders, we'll find you and kill you - no questions asked."

Dexter stared at the keys like they were a foreign object. He glanced at John, who had ignored the instructions and was wiping clean his fingers after finishing his tacos and chips. "You have time to eat nine tacos but ignore the Russians when they kidnap Lilly?"

"I was hungry, what can I say? She'll be fine," John said, slurping down the rest of his Coke.

The three men in suits and Lilly peeled out of the parking lot in a black SUV. Dexter watched the restaurant workers yelling at each other in Spanish. He apologized, waved John to leave, and entered the Prius. "What the hell just happened?" Dexter asked.

"What's wrong with this car? I drive a Ford F-150 and I could fit this car in the extended cab. Is this car for little people?" John said, pressing the passenger seat lever to push the seat almost into the backseat.

Dexter jammed in the keys and fired up the car. "This car sounds like a sewing machine. No way I'm keeping up with that SUV."

Dexter hit the gas and peeled out of the Casa Sanchez parking lot, turning onto Broadway. He wasn't sure where the SUV had turned as he scanned the busy road with passing cars on each side of the urban street.

"What's the plan boss? You heading back to the hotel? I wouldn't try nothing funny or we might sleep in a box six feet under," John said, licking salsa from his fingers.

Dexter stared out into the busy LA streets and didn't acknowledge John. He looked left and then right. "Lilly is sleeping with Boris. Boris is running some weird movie studio manipulating young girls. Selling them false dreams. He's a cheating Russian man-whore and somehow we're caught in the middle. Oh yeah, and Pope is a liar and a whore too. Did I miss anything?"

"Sounds about right. I wouldn't chase those Russians for two reasons. One, this car hasn't got the horses. Two, what you just said. These Russians are up to something dark. Let's do what they told us. Go to the hotel, find Boris, get our money, and head home and have a beer at O'Malley's. Oh yeah, and not die. I'd like to live to at least find Mrs. Woods."

The one thing Dexter wouldn't do... didn't know how to do... and couldn't do... was stand down from a fight. Maybe it's why he loved the side job more than he should've. And maybe it's why he ran his own business. He wasn't a rule follower. No Russians would tell him what to do.

"We will not die. I just need a second to thin—" Dexter's words hung in the air, "Yep, that's it. We're doing that."

"Dexter please tell me what's up. We headed back to the hotel? Like the large Russians told us in the restaurant."

"Remember you were too busy eating tacos to even acknowledge the Russians. But I have a better idea. Need to chat with someone. I think she can help."

Dexter hung a left and headed toward the one ten. After driving on the highway for a while he exited onto the one. The ocean air blew through the opened driver window. Dexter and John rolled into the Palos Verdes Manor Assisted Living facility. The friendly guard opened a sliding window.

"Hey fellas. How can I help you?"

"I'd like to visit Mrs. Pope."

The security guard took a double take at Dexter. He wrote out two visitor tags. "Were you here a few days ago with Jake?"

"Yes, I was. I'm back to see Mrs. Pope as she's not doing well. It's the least I can do for the family."

"You're family?"

"Distant. But family is family, right?"

"You can't choose em', but it's all we got."

The security guard slapped two visitor passes in Dexter's hand and opened the arm on the security shack. "Say hello to Mrs. Pope. Tell her I hope she feels better soon."

"Will do," Dexter said, and drove up the drive to the visitor parking lot.

"Dexter... not to be the skeptical one. Why are we at an old-people's home? I don't do well with the smell of pee. My grandma was in one of these places and it made me sad. Trapped in this place and not sure why," John said, glancing out the passenger window.

"If one person can help us get answers, it's Pope's mom."

"Pope's mom's going to help us?"

"I don't know. But we've found ourselves alone in So Cal with few contacts. She might be our only hope of getting home not in a body bag."

"I don't know, Dex. I don't like the body bag talk. Mrs. Woods is out there. We should've listened to the Russians. Won't this make things worse?"

Dexter exited the Prius and straightened his John Deere hat. "You come up with an idea and I'll listen. Until then, let's go."

16

Dexter and John rode the elevator up to Room 307. Dexter knocked on the door. He whispered to John. "Just follow my lead and stay cool."

Mrs. Pope opened the door. She took a moment to recognize Dexter. "Is that you Dexter? It's good to see you again. Where's Jakey?"

"He's not here today. I brought my friend John. He's from out of town."

"Why bring him here? This place is depressing."

"That's what I—" John said.

Dexter elbowed him in the stomach. "I wanted to make sure you were doing okay. How are you today?"

Mrs. Pope waved the boys into the small apartment. They sat on the couch and Dexter felt a sense of deja vu. "Any luck finding Jim?" Mrs. Pope asked.

"That's why we're here. I wanted to ask some more questions."

She glanced at the floor and fiddled with a Reader's Digest on the end table. "I apologize for my little spell when you were here. The news about my husband must've been too much to handle. I'm doing much better. How can I help?"

Dexter waved it off and glanced at John, who was taking in all the background information. "Thanks for your support. Well, uh, let's say the case seems to get more complicated by the minute. Can you tell us more about Jim? Anything that would tie him to the Russian mob?"

"A mob? Oh heavens, no. Are Russians after him?" she said, in a sweet tone.

Dexter shrugged. "Doing everything we can. But we have associated Jim with a Russian crime outfit in LA."

"I'm getting calls from the hospital about my bills. Jake's supposed to be taking care of them. Is everything okay?"

Dexter stumbled over the question. Pope wasn't exactly who he appeared to be. He could be dead, for all they knew. "He's fine. Has Jake called or visited since the last time we talked?"

Mrs. Pope grabbed her temples and shook her head. "The ole' mind isn't sharp like it used to be. Come to think of it... He was here yesterday. Jake had a pretty blonde girl with him. Said they were serious. Few girls have shown interest in Jake lately. But now he's found the love of his life. I'd give anything to have grand babies before the cancer takes me home."

"Don't sell your son's love life short," Dexter said.

"What's that son?"

"Nothing. Did you catch the name of the girl?"

Mrs. Pope sat in silence and worked on the questions like she was solving a math equation. "The chemo and radiation gives me cancer brain. Linda... Lilith... Lilly?"

"Did you say Lilly?" John asked.

"Yeah, that's it, Lilly. Sweet girl. She's an actress."

John grabbed Dexter on the knee and squeezed. Is Lilly sleeping with everyone in LA, Dexter thought to himself.

"You're sure it was Lilly? Not Linda or some other name? She was here yesterday, with Jake?"

Mrs. Pope nodded.

"Did they say where they were going? What they were up to?"

"Nothing too exciting. Something about Lilly going to a film shoot. I'm sorry boys, my memory is foggy."

Dexter yanked out a notepad and took a couple notes. He wanted to make sure he was getting all the details straight. The vastness of LA was making him confused for most of the trip. When you hunt down bad guys in LeClaire, there's only so many places they can hide. LA was a different story.

"No problem ma'am," Dexter said, trying to reassure Mrs. Pope despite her fuzzy memory. "Every bit helps for getting closer to solving the case. What was the mood of Jake? Did he seem happy, angry, nervous?"

Mrs. Pope raised her frail pointer finger. "One thing I remember is he appeared nervous. He dropped a glass which wasn't normal. And he was shaking and had a hard time getting his words out. Nervous is a good word to describe him."

Dexter scribbled on the notepad.

"Did Jake mention anything that would make him stressed? Nervous?"

"Something related to work. His boss was giving him a hard time. Which is odd because Jake has his own company."

"You know for sure?"

"What? The PI business? I guess Jake could be lying about it. But he's talked about it in the past. I've never visited his offices because of my illness. I'm not sure why he'd lie about his work. He doesn't make much money. Stressed all the time."

"Aren't we all?" John said.

Dexter scribbled a note on his pad. "I have another question which might seem strange."

Mrs. Pope smiled, "When you're my age and you've seen it all, no question is off limits. Please ask anything, I want to help where I can."

"Has Jake ever mentioned working at a movie studio?"

Mrs. Pope took a couple beats. It surprised Dexter that she didn't give a quick no. "He has. Not directly. Jake wanted to be in the film business. He did some theater in high school and took some auditions in his early twenties. Nothing ever came. He went into law enforcement instead. Applied for the LAPD police academy and got in. Proudest day of his life."

Dexter nodded. "Has Jake done any acting in the last couple of years? Mention any local community theater or auditions?"

"Jake's too busy with his police work. Anything is possible, I guess. How are these questions going to help your case? Is Jake acting again?"

"Not sure. He's connected to a local film studio in LA," Dexter said, and sighed, trying to get the courage up to ask another weird question, "Does Jake hang out with any Russians?"

"Russians? First Jim, now Jake. Now that's a weird question. Is Jake's girlfriend a Russian mail-order bride or something? Few girls calling of late. Is that why they're getting married so fast? People on the internet are getting hitched all the time."

Dexter and John laughed. "No ma'am. We have spotted

Jake hanging around some Russian dudes. They aren't the nicest people. Dumb question..."

"Not a dumb question. Come to think of it, he talks about his trainer at the gym. How he's helped Jake get into the best shape of his life. I think he's a Russian."

"Name?"

"Uncertain. I'm sure Jake said he was a Russian. Does that help?"

"Yes ma'am, helps a ton."

"Good. Anything else I can help with? If not, I need a nap. Sorry to be rude. But if I don't nap you'll see a side of me that's not pleasant."

Dexter and John understood and said their goodbyes, and left the apartment.

They punched the buttons to the elevator and waited for the doors to open. "I think Jake's role with the Russians goes deep. The only Russian so far is Boris, and the meatheads trying to hold us hostage at the hotel. Pope acted like he barely knew Boris. But I think they're working together."

John nodded, as he wasn't as informed on the case as Dexter. The doors opened. Two men in suits stood with their arms crossed, and they were wearing dark shades. "You having a nice field trip boys? I thought we were clear on you heading back to the motel. This will not make the bosses happy."

Dexter glanced at John and gave him a nod. "I don't give a shit about your bosses."

Dexter yanked a pistol from the back of his jeans and pistol-whipped the Russian on the right temple with the butt of the gun. He crumpled into the corner of the elevator car.

The second Russian lurched at John. He grabbed the Russian around the chest and squeezed. John was not fit, but he was stronger than an ox. He gripped the Russian harder and harder until he couldn't breathe. He slid down next to the other Russian and wasn't making a sound.

Dexter and John exited the elevator, scaled the stairs down to the parking lot, and sat in the Prius.

Dexter said, "These Russians are watching our every move. This will make things tricky. We need to find Jake. If Jake and Lilly are an item something's not Kosher."

"I don't know Dex. We should've listened to the Russians. I'm a lover, not a fighter."

"You did good in the elevator. Trust me. We're not going down without a fight. These Russians might be city rats, but they've never run into country power."

17

Dexter raced down Sunset Blvd, glancing in the rear view of the Prius. He was sure Russians were on their tail and their next steps weren't exactly clear. Pope's association with Boris was confusing and his relationship with Lilly made everything in Dexter's mind a blur.

Dexter slapped the steering wheel. "Dammit, Pope. Would you ever think he'd be such a douche bag? In LeClaire he seemed like a normal guy. I don't what kind of shit he has found himself in... but I don't like. Now we're caught in the middle of his lies."

"It'll work out Dex, it always does. You'll think of something."

John was always the voice of reason and trusted Dexter to find the solutions he often lacked. They had been friends since life's first cries and worked well together. Dexter the cowboy and free spirit, and John the commonsense one. But Dexter needed a plan.

"Why don't we head to the hotel? Gather our thoughts and not make things a bigger mess than they need to be."

"Not an option. The Russians know we're rogue. We go back to the hotel and we walk into a firing squad."

"How do you know? These Russians could be all talk. We go back to the hotel and use our negotiating skills. They hired us to complete the job. If they don't want our services, the hell with them and we bounce."

John smirked and appreciated the positive outlook of Dexter despite his crazy idea. "No way. We're already skating on thin ice. I don't want to catch a Russian having a bad day who then slaughters our families. I'm not living with that kind of guilt."

"If we're dead it won't matter," Dexter said, giving John a glance in the passenger seat, "We don't bow to no one."

"Where do you suggest we go? This city is frighteningly busy and we don't know a soul except Pope's mom, Pope, and well, that's it."

Dexter slapped the steering wheel again and glanced out of the Prius window, watching the seas of cars rush by. "Damn this forsaken place. You can't get a decent meal in this town. Think Dexter... think..."

Dexter yanked on the wheel of the Prius and John's face plastered to the side of the passenger window. "What the hell, bro!"

"I got an idea. We visit LAPD."

"Worst idea ever. You're going to walk into the authorities after the mess we're in."

"Yep. Before you got here, we found a girl who committed suicide. But it was a murder. Pope dated her. We go undercover to the LAPD and get more info on the case."

John slapped his pudgy forehead. "Wait a minute. Pope dated a girl who committed suicide? And you think it was a murder? Who is this guy?"

"He lied about knowing her when we checked out a lead. I saw a picture of them together in the bedroom."

"Good work, Sherlock. So how do you plan to walk into a police station and not cause a ruckus?"

"Disguises."

"What is this, Scooby Doo?"

"We do what we have to do. Yaba Dabba Doo!"

Dexter played with his phone and typed "costume shops" in the search bar. "We're in Hollywood. There's gotta be somewhere we can get some disguises, right?"

"What do you imagine we dress as? I'm not in the best shape right now. I'm carrying a little holiday weight."

Dexter slapped John in his jiggly belly. "What holiday? Thanksgiving 1986?"

"Hey, I'm sensitive about my weight. It's genetic."

"Yeah... a diet of Hot Pockets and Twinkies has nothing to do with your DNA. Relax. We'll find a disguise to fit your hefty frame."

Dexter slammed the Prius into park in front of Make Believe, Inc., off Pico Blvd. Dexter glanced at his phone. "Yelp gave it some good reviews. Lots of inventory."

The boys strolled into the costume shop and a flamboyant man behind the counter lit up with a smile. He took a second glance at John. "I like the big ones," the man said, licking his lips.

"Excuse me? I don't appreciate the fat jokes."

"That's not a joke honey," he said, taking a peek at Dexter. "How can I help you strong men?"

Dexter watched a lady hang a Superman costume on the back wall behind the counter. He scanned the rows of costumes. "I need a man-bun. You have any man-buns?"

John stared at Dexter and had no idea what he was talking about. "You want to explain, boss?"

"It's a California thing. Dudes putting their hair up in a bun. Like how our moms used to wear them back in the day. Not my thing but it might work. What do you think?" Dexter said to the man behind the counter.

"What do you need it for? It's not a hot seller."

"Is that because every dude in Venice already has one?" Dexter asked.

The man paused. "Maybe."

"It's for a costume party. We're not from around here. Missouri, to be exact."

"Ooh, I like country boys."

"Not everyone from Missouri is a country boy. But we are..."

Dexter tipped his John Deere hat, and John gave a weak wave.

The feminine man with a tank top and slicked hair nodded. "I like men from the hills."

"Missouri is mostly flat. I think you like *all* men," John said.

Dexter elbowed John in the side. He whispered, "Shut up," and then looked at the man behind the counter, "Don't listen to my fat friend. Give us a couple man-buns. One that'll fit my friend's giant noggin. Why don't we do blonde and black?"

The man tossed the wads of hair on the counter. "Try these on. Make sure they're snug."

John looked at Dexter with angry eyes. He tried on the man-bun and gave it a couple tugs. "You better have the best plan ever dreamed up. If I get killed wearing this thing you'll have to answer to my mother."

Dexter tried his man-bun on and gave it a snap in place. He walked to a mirror on the counter. "These are horrendous. Why would a grown man want one of these?"

Dexter grabbed some new sunglasses and a flannel shirt. "No one will know we're country boys from LeClaire. We look like authentic hipsters from So Cal," Dexter said, strutting around the store.

John sighed. "Definitely going to get killed."

Dexter paid up.

The owner of the store gave a wave and blew a kiss. Dexter gave an awkward half smile and sped up his pace to the car.

The boys headed to the LAPD offices with man-buns securely in place and itchy flannel shirts secured.

"This better work boss. Might be the most uncomfortable I've felt since eating that extra-large pizza in one sitting."

"Follow my lead and don't say a thing."

The LAPD headquarters had a visitor lot near the entrance. Dexter parked the Prius and yanked out his phone from his jean pocket. "One second," Dexter said to John, and dialed the phone.

"Hello, yes. My name is detective Ron Black. I've been working undercover on a case for a few months. We ran into a snag when one of our suspects came up dead. Can I speak to someone who handles open cases?"

The receptionist transferred Dexter to the homicide department. John slapped Dexter in the side of the head. "What are you doing?"

Dexter covered the phone. "I'm doing some leg work before we head inside. Trust me."

John shook his head.

"Yes, my name is Ron Black. I was working a case undercover for a few months. They found our suspect dead. Her name was Jill Morris. They said it was suicide. Do you have any more information on the case?"

"Who's Jill?" John asked.

"Don't worry about it," Dexter said, trying to work double duty talking to the person on the phone.

The person came on the phone. "Who is this? Did you say Ron Black? Are you an LAPD detective? The name doesn't sound familiar."

"No, I'm not LAPD. Jill was under FBI investigation and we were following her undercover. Did you find anything else out?"

There was a pause on the phone. "My file says coroner found the body not to be consistent with a suicide. Someone strangled her."

"Too bad. That means the killer's still on the loose. I guess we'll get back to work. Thanks for the time," Dexter said, and hung up the phone.

"What are you doing? You can't call LAPD and say you're FBI. You're going to get us in trouble."

"Any better ideas? Remember, you come up with an idea, I back down."

"Who is this Jill person?"

"Pope killed her."

"What?"

"I don't know for sure. That's my guess. Pope was sleeping with her and we found her dead. He lied about knowing her. I'm sure he did it."

"Pope is a douche, yes. But don't jump to conclusions. Innocent until proven guilty in my book," John said.

"If it isn't Pope, someone wanted her dead. I think Jill's connected to Pope, Boris, Pope's dad, and the Russians. Just not sure how yet."

"Look at you. You sound like a real detective."

Dexter exited the Prius. "Not just a pretty face, my chubby friend. Now we go into the offices."

"Are you sure? This man-bun is giving me a rash."

"Don't ask questions. This is part two of the plan."

18

Dexter explained the plan to John as they walked to the entrance of the LAPD offices. John thought Dexter was crazy for entering a building full of cops. Not to mention they were dressed with man-buns and itchy flannel shirts. Dexter said it was to fit in, John felt they stuck out like a sore thumb.

Dexter stood at the automatic sliding doors to the entrance of the offices. "I learned a fun fact last year."

"What's that? Mrs. Peppers who owns the beauty salon is a man?"

Dexter waved off the comment. "Everyone knows that."

John gave a weak smile and pretended he knew. "Yeah, of course, common knowledge."

"Police reports are often public record. Depends on the region and county. We're going to check on the Jill Morris case and see what we can find. Nothing to worry about."

"The dead chick?"

"Yes, the dead chick. The one Pope killed. We take him down and the rest of the Russians follow. That's my hunch."

"Why you so sure Pope's a head guy of the organization?

He sounds more like a lonely dude who can't keep it in his pants. He doesn't strike me as a Russian Kingpin."

"Don't let the laid back city boy from So Cal fool you. Everything in me says Pope's up to no good. He's a liar and has been stringing me along since I got here. Using us to do his dirty work. He wants us to take the fall. Not today..."

A pair of officers strolled by, giving the men a glance. They smirked.

Dexter played it off and adjusted the man-bun, and gave a weak smile.

"So your brilliant plan is ridiculous consumes and waltzing into a building full of people who can throw us in jail," John said, adjusting his sagging man-bun.

"Follow my lead and keep quiet."

John pretended to zip his lip. "If we're thrown in jail, I get the bottom bunk."

"Calm down. We're not the murderers. Just a couple hill-billies on a vacation, remember?"

"Sure. But two hillbillies getting mixed up in official police work and solving crimes off the clock needs to stay a secret. I'd like to get married someday. Not locked up with your dumb ass because you thought man-buns were a good idea."

Dexter ignored the comment and nodded for John to enter the sliding doors to the LAPD building. "Like I said, keep quiet, let me do the talking. And your man-bun looks great."

Dexter glanced to a couple signs hanging in the lobby of the LAPD. He found a front receptionist who pointed the boys to an office to the right. They entered a second set of doors and asked another receptionist what to do. She told them to sit down and wait for an officer.

John's stomach rumbled and Dexter tapped his legs on

the floor. A heavyset man wearing a grey suit with a receding hairline waved them into his office. He shut the door.

The officer slumped into his chair and twiddled his thumbs. He apparently had better things to do. "How can I help you boys today?" he said, locking eyes on John's blonde man-bun.

"Thank you for the time. Officer Fields is it?" Dexter said, reading his name tag.

"Yes. Thirty years on the force."

"Thank you for serving the fine people of LA," John said.

"Not all of them are fine. I'd be out of work if that were the case. What can I do for you?"

He leaned back in his office chair and sipped on a coffee.

"Well, Detective Fields, you have a front row seat to the worst things people do to one another. You probably see death every day."

"How much time you have? I could tell you stories."

"My brother and I came here today under less than ideal circumstances. Our sister has died."

The officer glanced at John and back at Dexter. "I'm sorry for your loss. Is our department involved?"

"Yes, sir. Not in her death, of course," Dexter said, with a smile, "She was found in her apartment. Your investigators came by the house to work the case."

"What was her name?"

"Jill Morris."

The officer leaned in front of his desk, fired on his computer, and tapped on the keys. "Let me look her up. Jill Morris, right?"

Dexter nodded.

Dexter and John sat in the sterile office and a world of nerves swirled in the air. John was pessimistic about how well Dexter's plan would work. He glanced at a bookshelf with a sea of trophies. "What are those trophies for?" John asked, as the detective tapped on the keyboard.

Dexter gave John an eye as he didn't want him talking and ruining the plan. John's curiosity often got them in trouble. "Nothing special. Some awards from the Mayor's office for protecting our citizens. A trophy for the department softball team. I was the pitcher."

"I used to play some ball. High school football. Not in game shape anymore but I could put a hurt on some fools," John said, jiggling his stomach.

The officer glanced up from his tapping on the computer and laughed. He grabbed his gut. "I'm with you. The reason I play soft pitch softball isn't for the exercise. More for the beer and pizza afterwards."

"Amen," John said, looking for a high five.

Dexter gave John a glance that was not a pleasant one. He whispered, "No more talking. Don't ruin this."

John scanned the rest of the office and folded his hands.

The officer laid back in his leather swivel chair. "I found Jill's file. Again, sorry for your loss. The case is still under investigation. Some details yet to be ironed out. I guess I'm confused about why you're here. Is there something else? Any information that might help the case?"

Dexter hesitated and gathered his words. He tried to fake a tear and laid his head on the desk. He peeked up at the officer. "This might sound strange. Our father was in law enforcement. Jilly, it's what we called her, was hoping to be a lawyer. She had sent in her application for law school and was getting ready to start in the fall. Law and justice always inspired her. Do you think..."

The officer was softening at the contrived story of Dexter. "What is it son? How can I help?"

"Something fascinated Jill with the ins and outs of law enforcement. I remember her telling me once that police reports were public record. It would mean a lot to have a copy of her case file. I don't want to read it. Our family was thinking about putting the report inside her coffin. I know it's weird," Dexter said, wiping a tear, and laying his head back on the desk.

The officer played with the mouse on his desk and hit a couple more keys. "Not a problem, consider it done. I rarely do this without some ID. It will be our secret. I know after working with hundreds of families that people grieve in different ways. The case is still open and we need more evidence before it's closed. But you take this copy and grieve with your family."

Dexter slowly lifted his head, wiped his face again, and gave John a sheepish grin. "Did you say the case is open?"

The officer leaned in and whispered. "I'm not supposed to do this... but I know you're going through a rough patch. There are some confusing details in the case we can't figure out. The original thought is your sister committed suicide. Now we don't think so."

"Did someone kill..."

The detective nodded.

"Oh, no, why God?" Dexter shouted out.

"I'm sorry, son. Would you know of anyone that might've wanted to hurt your sister?"

"No, sir. All she wanted was to be the best lawyer in LA. Make sure the bad guys were taken off the streets. That was her life's mission. We thought she took her life because of the pressure of law school and not wanting to fail."

The detective shook his head and grabbed his temple. "Man, Jill sounds like a wonderful person."

A printer buzzed at the side of the officer's desk. He

grabbed a piece of paper and slid it across the wide desk. The detective took out a black pen and crossed a few things out. "Here are the reports, boys. I crossed out some details. The case is still open and I have to protect the innocent until proven guilty."

As he slid the paper across the desk, he took a second glance. He turned the paper around. "Come to think of it, I didn't see you boys names on the report. Did a detective come and talk to you about your sister? If they didn't, we haven't done our job."

John squirmed in his chair and a bead of sweat formed on his temple. He tapped his legs up and down. "Nope. No officers talked to us. We weren't that close to Jill," John said.

Dexter interjected, "What my brother meant to say is we weren't close the last year. Jill was preparing for law school and we had a business to run. We're a close family," Dexter said, pinching a lump of John's flabby leg.

The officer gave a confused look at the boys. "Are you sure there's nothing you want to share to help the investigation? Anyone we should talk to?"

Dexter grabbed a copy of the police report and read it over, mouthing the words. "Something on the report caught my eye."

The officer leaned over the edge of the desk and stared at the report. He took a second look. "What did you see, son?"

Dexter pointed at a drawing and a note written by one officer at the crime scene. "These pictures. Were these significant for the case?"

The officer read the note on the report and glanced back at Dexter. He seemed to be intrigued by the question of Dexter. "An officer found photos in the bedroom. Potential suspects."

"Does it say who the people were?"

"I'm sorry boys. I can't share that information. I crossed out the names."

Dexter worked on a tear. He sighed. "I understand. But it would mean a lot to my sister to know everything is being done to find her killer."

The officer looked at John and back at Dexter. He leaned back in his chair and whispered again. "Okay... I'm getting close to retirement. When you get to my age, sometimes you have to do what you feel is right. I like you boys. The photos haven't been confirmed. We're working on the details. Think one of these guys might be the killer."

Dexter paused, nodded, and took a deep breath. "We can't bring my sister back from the dead. Nothing will ever erase the memories we had with Jilly. But I might know the people in the photos."

"Do you have a name?"

"Jake Pope. He was her boyfriend for a time. I'd try to find him. He might be the clue you're looking for."

The officer wrote Jake's name on a sticky note and smiled. He slid the police report back to Dexter on the desk. "Take this report and may you find healing. I'm sorry for your loss. You have helped many people today, including your sister," he slid a business card across the desk, "Call me if you have any more information. We'll do everything we can to make your sister proud. Take those bad guys off the streets."

Dexter gave praying hands and rose to his feet. He waved to John to follow him out of the office. He gave the officer a handshake. "My brother and I are impressed by this fine institution. The LAPD must be the finest department in the land if it takes care of her citizens in this manner."

"We try. God bless and let us know if there's anything else we can do?"

"Get Jilly's killer..."

Dexter and John left the LAPD building and sat in the Prius. They both took off their man-buns and gave a sigh of relief. This might be their only hope of leaving LA alive.

19

John and Dexter hummed along Highway 101 feeling a sense of momentum after the visit to the LAPD. The generous mood of the detective happened to be the break the guys needed. John was impressed with Dexter's idea of fooling the officer into getting the report and trapping Pope. John hated it when Dexter's plans worked.

"Nice move back there," John said, sipping on a Diet Cherry Coke, "I'll admit that took some huge balls to pull that off."

"Sometimes desperation calls for asking for what you want. If the detective follows up with Jake Pope one of our problems will go away. Cut off the head of the snake, right?"

John nodded and sipped his thirty-two ounce soda. "So let me get things straight. Roger Morris is the father of Jill, who was murdered. Pope is holding the smoking gun? Boris Popov is a Russian personal trainer who's gone missing and also the head of a Russian film studio spreading a message of God knows what. And it somehow ties into Pope's dad, who's missing. Am I tracking?"

"Let's not forget about Jake Pope. He comes to LeClaire after the LAPD give him a timeout for his attitude. The department later fires him. He starts his own PI business and now is connected to the Russians. Not to mention a compulsive liar and sleeping with every girl in Venice."

John sat in the Prius and took in all the information. "Sounds like a dumpster fire. My stomach hurts processing this stuff. Why can't we leave?"

Dexter liked the idea but something in his gut was telling him these Russians were not messing around. The men who showed up at Pope's mother's assisted living facility gave Dexter confidence these guys were watching their every move. If the Russians and Pope were telling the truth, the potential for Dexter's and John's families being harmed was too much for Dexter to take.

"Running's an option. But that's how we used to handle things. Not now. If these guys are serious and our families are in danger, we keep riding the horse until she bucks. We need to ride a little longer."

"Is ratting out Pope a good idea?" John asked.

"Time will tell. But I figure unless the Russians are watching the cops we're okay. Let the cops take down Pope and we stay out of it."

John nodded and sipped more of his soda. "So I guess the bigger question becomes: what now? We're driving around So Cal and don't have a next move."

Dexter held up the police report. "We aren't totally in the dark. We visit a key witness on the report. See what else we can find. I snapped a picture on my phone before the detective crossed out the names."

John gave a fist bump. "Nice... Dex. No man-buns, right?"

"Nope, that'll stay in the vault."

Dexter handed John his phone and asked him to read off the names of the witnesses and the addresses. It appeared Harrison Barber lived near Jill Morris. "Harrison was a close neighbor. Maybe he can tell us about Jill and if he saw Pope hanging around."

Dexter punched the address into his phone and arrived at the apartment complex ten minutes later. John wouldn't make it without food so Dexter found a Wendy's. John said it made him think of home because LeClaire had minimal options for *good food made quickly.*

They sat in front of the Shady Acres apartment complex where Jill and Harrison Barber lived. The California sun was setting and glowing yellow and red in the distance. A couple surfers strolled by with boards tucked under their arms. They looked like they could be related to Pope with their bleached blonde hair and tanned skin. "Don't see those in LeClaire," John said, watching the young men walk by and disappear up the street.

The apartment of Harrison Barber was on the bottom floor below Jill's. If anyone had seen anything, Harrison was a good bet. The boys walked along a path past Jill's apartment. Dexter paused and glanced up to see a police tape still tied to the front door of Jill's place. "Sad," Dexter said to John, as they continued up the path.

Barber's place was dead, except for a happy mutt jumping on the couch in the front window. Dexter gave a firm rap on the door.

They waited.

He gave another knock and heard a raspy voice yell at the dog, telling it to shut the hell up.

The door opened and an unshaven man in a robe emerged. "Better not be no damn Jehovah's Witness. I walked the aisle in the Baptist church forty years ago and don't need to be part of no cult."

A combination of three-day-old wet gym socks mixed with a dirty dog smells punched the guys in the face. "No, sir. No cults here. We're card carrying Baptists but are here on other business. Can we have a minute of your time? Like to talk about Jill Morris, the girl who lived above you," Dexter said, pointing to Jill's apartment.

The man in the bathrobe scratched his crotch, gave the boys a look up and down, and snorted. "I guess so. Sad what happened to that girl. Hurry up because Judge Judy is coming on and I never miss an episode."

It surprised Dexter that the man invited them into his small apartment. The boys found a brown couch covered in cat hair. The man slumped into a Lazy Boy. He lit up a cigarette. "You guys don't look like cops. From around here?"

"No, sir. We're law enforcement from another department helping a colleague out. It's common practice when offices get overloaded with cases. LA's a hotbed for crime," Dexter said, trying not to touch the couch.

"It's a shit hole if you ask me. Fires burning houses down. Expensive to live. Traffic. Girls getting killed in their apartments for no reason. If I didn't have cheap rent, I'd have been gone long ago. Can't live on no fixed military retirement. No respect for our troops," the man said, taking a long drag on the cigarette.

"When did you serve?" John asked.

"Vietnam, 301st Airborne. Baddest infantry in Nam. America don't make tough guys anymore. A bunch of pussies wearing man-buns."

Dexter and John smirked. "Amen brother, the amount of man-buns in this town is criminal," John said.

Dexter tried to change the conversation as the smells in

the apartment were making his stomach hurt. "So, Mr. Barber. Can you tell us about Jill Morris? Did you know her well?"

The tone of Barber changed. He averted his eyes and stared into the distance. "She was a sweet girl and used to help me out time to time. Fed the cats and dog when I was out of town. Always friendly and wearing a smile. It's a shame what happened to her. Good thing I'm a praying man or I might've done something I'd regret if I ever found that dirt bag."

Dexter glanced at John and asked another question. "Do you know how she died?"

"I was talking to one of those LAPD detectives who came around after the incident. They said something about a suicide. No way Jill killed herself. She was the most positive person I ever met. Someone killed her, I'm sure," Barber said, shaking his head, and taking another drag on the cigarette.

Dexter said, "Jill seemed like a great girl. Did you ever see anyone hanging around the apartment? Was she in a relationship?"

"Dudes were coming around here all the time. Jill was a sweet girl... maybe too sweet."

"Any guy stand out in your mind?"

Barber took a long hit on the cigarette and paused a couple beats. "A surfer dude came around. Thirties, blonde, tan."

"Did you catch a name?"

"None of my business. But he gave me dirty looks whenever I saw him headed up to her apartment. Like he was better than me. Come to think of it... most of the guys did the same thing."

"Most of the guys? Tell me more."

"Like I said, Jill was a sweet girl, maybe too sweet. Some well-built man came by a lot. He had a funny accent."

"Russian?"

"Some kind of foreigner. He came over all hours of the night."

Dexter's mind was spinning as he thought about Pope and Boris coming over to Jill's house. Pope made sense if they were an item. But what was Boris doing there? Maybe Jill was too sweet, but why?

Dexter pulled out his notepad. "Can you tell me more about the dark-haired guy?"

"Dark hair, tall, and good shape. Must've spent a lot of time in the gym. He had creepy brown eyes. Reminded me of Charlie in Nam."

"Charlie?" John asked.

"Those sons of bitches in Vietnam who killed all our soldiers."

John nodded and didn't want to engage further.

Dexter asked, "How much do you remember about the night Jill died? Did you have any interaction with her?"

"Funny you should ask," Barber said, as he smashed his cigarette in his coffee cup, "The night Jill died she came over and gave me some chocolate chip cookies. She could bake her ass off."

"Did Jill seem okay?"

"She was her typical happy self. Always concerned about other people. Those cookies were damn good, too."

"Nothing that would indicate depression? Struggling with something?"

He shook his head. "Nothing, man. Jill was steady Eddy. I know we weren't best friends, and I didn't spend every minute with her. But if she had mental problems she didn't show it."

"Anything else you want to tell us? I know Judge Judy is coming on soon and don't want to take all your time," Dexter said, giving John a grin.

Barber slapped his thigh, making his robe flip up into the air. He leaned on the edge of the Lazy Boy. "All this suicide talk is bullshit. Cops don't know what the hell they're saying. Late that night a car pulled up in front of the apartments. I was watching TV in the living room and heard voices coming from the stairs leading up to Jill's apartment. A guy yelled, and a woman was crying. I assume it was Jill."

"What happened next?" John asked, intrigued with Barber's new revelation.

"Thumping on the ceiling and more screaming. The screen door slammed open and someone ran down the stairs to the car. It sped off, and that was it."

Barber lit another cigarette and his face turned solemn. He wasn't crying but something in his face said a deep sadness was inside him. "You okay Mr. Barber? It sounds like you and Jill were close. I know this is hard. We're almost done."

"I should've done more. When I heard the screaming and yelling. I should have done more…"

"Don't blame yourself. It's hard to know what to do in these situations."

"Shit, I was in Vietnam kid. I've run through the jungles and saved my men from dying in the bush. The least I could've done was check on Jill. Dammit. The stuff I taught my men about being heroic. I guess I didn't take my own advice."

Dexter rose from the couch and stuck out a hand. "Mr. Barber, we thank you for the time. I'm sorry for you losing a good neighbor. But we'll keep working the case and find Jill's killer."

Barber stayed seated, nodded, and finished his second cigarette. "Thanks, boys. Sorry I wasn't much help. Let me know if you need anything? I like you boys. Those other detectives rubbed me the wrong way."

Dexter thanked him again and exited the smelly apartment with John. They sat in the car for a moment and Dexter reflected on the conversation. No way Jill's death was a suicide. Not after talking with Barber. Everything pointed to Pope but the mystery man, maybe a Russian; was making things interesting.

Jill might've been sweet, too sweet. But Dexter believed Pope was the culprit of her death, but why?

Dexter fired up the Prius and John nodded off in the passenger seat. Dexter glanced into the rearview mirror and saw a black SUV parked behind them.

Someone was watching them.

20

A man with dark shades and a black suit came up next to the Prius. He had a thick Russian accent. He tapped on the driver window. Dexter rolled the window down. "Can we help you?"

The Russian gave a smirk. He lifted the side of his suit jacket and revealed a pistol jammed in his belt. "We had a deal. You listen to our directions and no-one gets hurt. What are you doing here?"

Dexter wasn't sure if the Russian was trying to trap him into saying something he'd regret. Had they been following him the entire time? Dexter and John weren't stupid in police work. They kept an eye on their surroundings the best they could, and were certain they weren't being tailed. Dexter gave a vague answer.

"Not sure what you mean? We have a friend at the apartments. Came to say hello. Is that a crime?"

"We're not dumb, Missouri. Why would you have friends in LA?" the Russians said, watching a motorcycle squeeze by on the narrow street.

"Okay, you caught us. We have no friends in this town

unless you count yourself," Dexter said, giving a thumb up to the Russian who wasn't amused with the comment. "My friend John is lonely. He hasn't been with a woman since high school. Thought I'd help him out," Dexter said.

The Russian turned back to stare at the Shady Acre Apartments sign. "They have hookers in there?"

"You'll have to see for yourself. LA's a lonely town and we all have needs, am I right?"

The Russian ignored the comment and glanced a second time at the apartments. He bent down and got in the face of Dexter. "I don't care what you're doing here. Get back to the hotel or we remove fingers one by one," the Russian said, smashing Dexter's hand onto the base of the driver side window.

"Got it," Dexter said, sliding his hand back, and giving it a shake.

"Easy Ivan Drago. We'll head back. You don't need to hurt my friend. It's my fault. I was lonely," John said, from the passenger side of the Prius.

John felt a sting in the side of his temple as a second Russian had exited the SUV. He punched John in the head through the window. Because of John's large and chubby head it didn't phase him. "Shit... guys. We get it. Back to the hotel," John said, rubbing the side of his skull.

Dexter tried to hold back laughter.

John rubbed his face. "You have ice at the hotel?"

"No funny business. Next time you'll need more than ice," the Russian said.

Dexter pulled the Prius out of the spot and slammed on the brakes as a small compact car zoomed by on the tight street. The SUV missed slamming into the back of the Prius by an inch. Dexter gave a wave with the middle finger in the rearview mirror and pulled out again. The SUV tailed them the entire trip back to the hotel.

John rubbed the side of his face. "What now boss man? The Russians are pissed. I bet they tailed us to LAPD and Barber's."

Dexter shrugged and shook out his hand crushed by the car window. "I don't care. We work for ourselves. Do what we want, and go where we want. The Russians think they're holding all the cards. But these country boys ain't no pushovers."

"What about all the family talk? Saying you didn't want nothing happening to Sam and the kids. We're playing with fire. Play it cool, Dex. We don't know what these Russians are about. I don't want some Russian mob showing up at my house and killing my mother. She's a nag, but she's all I got."

Dexter stretched out his fingers and gripped the steering wheel. He watched the cars on the highway zoom in and out of lanes. "These California drivers are maniacs. You can't even get on the highway unless you're going eighty. Why in the hell is there traffic with seven lanes? Only traffic you see in LeClaire is when a Semi blows over a deer and goes into the ditch. We gotta get out of here. Road Rage a brewing."

"What's the plan? Sounds like Pope is a murderer, maybe Boris too. But why? Do we try to find them? I think if we find Boris we find Pope's dad. But I still don't understand the connection."

"Pope mentioned something about his dad buying a gym and getting mixed up with the Russians. It sounds like his dad pissed someone off and they might've taken it out on him. Pope and his dad have a weird relationship. I don't see a reason for Pope to care about finding Pops unless something else is going on. He said his dad had money and was helping pay for his mom's medical bills. You think that's true? Pope's doing okay if he's heading up a Russian operation. Shit, I don't know what to believe. Someone is lying their ass off, and we need to find who."

"Families are complicated. I don't know why we still love them after the shit they put us through. We aren't innocent, that's for sure. But why do the Russians want us to find Boris and Pope's dad? Who's behind this? The outsiders come to town and they want us to do their dirty work, but why?"

Dexter snapped back. "Damn, fatty. That's an angle I'd not considered. Why go to LeClaire and bring you to California to work for them? We're nothing special. Why not use some other local nobodies? Pope has something else up his sleeve."

The boys sat in silence as the Californian sun set over the 405 freeway. A ball of red and orange blinded them through the small window of the Prius.

"Let's go back to the hotel and get something to eat. My stomach is turning inside out. We've barely ate today. Lay low under the watch of the Russians and figure out our next steps. The longer we let these bastards control us... the harder it will be to leave," John said.

John rubbed his stomach. "We play it safe. Do what they want, find these assholes, and get our money and leave," John said.

"We don't lay down like that. Any good antique picker never goes for the first negotiation. We have negotiation power too. If this job was simple and they could get anyone to do it, why wouldn't they? Why go to the trouble to keep us around? We've already broken their trust and they keep giving us chances. Why?"

"Remember when your momma smacked your bottom as a kid. What did she say? Don't do it again or you get a whipping. Don't do it again, or your father will hear about it.

I don't want to wait for daddy to come home, the Russian version," John said.

Dexter nodded. A deep focus in his eyes like he was day-dreaming. John knew Dexter wasn't going to lay down easy. It wasn't in Dexter.

"True. Let's get some food and sleep on it," Dexter said.

The Prius pulled back into the Odessa Hotel. Dexter and John found their room and were surprised to find a gift in the room. Two plates of BBQ and a side of beans and cheesy corn.

How did they know?

21

Dexter and John devoured their BBQ in the hotel room and lay in their respective beds watching Russian TV. Dexter didn't want to like the BBQ because Missouri has the best. But, he did. He convinced himself that someone from Missouri shipped it here, or a Kansas City native was running a BBQ joint in the city.

John licked the remaining sauce residue off his chubby fingers. "Damn, boss. That BBQ stands up to anything in Missouri."

"Don't talk like that. It was okay... I've had better."

"You're telling me a slab from Joe's KC is better? A close second?"

"I'm not ready to crown some hipster BBQ joint best of the West. Calm down."

John folded his hands on his head and took a deep, satisfying sigh as his belly of BBQ settled. "You're in a mood."

Dexter played with the remote for the TV. "Sorry, I don't like these Russians buttering our bread. They know our weakness for BBQ. The vacation is over and we need to get to work," Dexter said, turning down the TV, "Here's an idea.

Pope's sleeping with a wannabe actress and working for the Russians. She ends up dead and Pope has egg on his face. Boris is hanging around the house with the same girl. What is the connection?"

John placed a finger over his lips and whispered. "Not too loud. This place could be tapped."

Dexter rolled his eyes.

"Let me ask another question. Why do you kill someone? Revenge? Or, because someone knows something that might get you in trouble? Maybe Jill had dirt on Pope, or Boris? They didn't want her to squeal so they killed her?"

Dexter found John's theory interesting. He switched to another channel on the TV. "What message would the Russians spread that Jill wanted to shut down? No one gives a damn about the Russians since the Cold War ended. The threat of nuclear bombs or World War III is old news. Would anyone take a group of crazy Russians seriously?"

"You lost me at Cold War. Who knows? They brainwash these girls none the less. You think the pull for fame is so strong in LA these girls would do anything? Even spread Russian nonsense?" John asked.

Dexter pondered the question for a second. "Maybe the Russians are getting payouts from a third party. The movie studio is a front for something else. These gullible girls wouldn't have a clue what was going on. They get on screen, make a few bucks, the Russians tell them it will look good on a resume, and everyone wins. I wonder if Jill found something out. After talking with Barber she seemed like a sharp girl."

John had dozed off from his BBQ hangover, "What was that boss? You say something?"

"Never mind chunky. Go back to sleep. It's what you do best."

Dexter rose from the bed and stood next to the TV. He cranked up the volume and watched a brunette read the teleprompter as she gave the news. A story about a Russian rock-and-roll group playing in the Ukraine. Dexter thought to himself that no way this channel was being broadcast to all of LA, unless there was some large Russian population that a dedicated channel would make sense. Something like the Spanish channel, Telemundo, where Dexter would watch the occasional soccer game in Missouri.

Dexter noticed a cable ran from the back of the TV to a jack in the wall. The cable looked out of place in Dexter's mind. It wasn't a power cable and looked more like something for the internet. He leaned behind the TV and examined a square logo with words written in red lettering.

Runet- an internet company.

Dexter knew AT&T, Comcast, and Google Fiber, but Runet was a new one. He thought nothing of it, as knowledge of internet providers wasn't his specialty. The bottom of the logo had an address on it. He typed it into his phone.

He watched the girls reading the news on the TV screen. Dexter glanced at the phone. Runet was an internet company that had an LA address. He searched the website and learned it had ties to Russia. Maybe the Russians were a big deal in La La Land after all?

Dexter ripped off his boot and flung it at John, who was snoring like a train. The boot caught him on the arm and John brushed it off like a fly on food at a summer picnic in Missouri. Dexter flung a second boot at John which caught him in the thigh.

Nothing.

Dead to the world.

Dexter headed to the bathroom and filled a plastic cup

with cold water. He dowsed John in the face on the bed. He sprung to life with fists clenched. "Who's there?"

"Wake up tub of lard. I found something."

"Come on, Dex. I need my beauty sleep. Wake a man after a plate of ribs you're bound to get yourself killed."

Dexter waved John to the TV. John wiped his eyes, scratched his groin, and sauntered to the TV. "Check out the logo on the back of the tube. You ever hear of that internet company?"

"Yeah, they're a Russian outfit."

"How'd you know?"

John was smart with technology and the latest gadgets. Stuff Dexter tried to steer clear of. But this was impressive to Dexter. "What else you know?"

"They're a big deal in technology over in Russia. I read about it on a website a couple years ago. They make billions of dollars. No other company like it in Russia."

"Once again, I underestimated your intelligence hiding under that chubby veneer."

"When you're in a dry season with the ladies, and extra time on your hands, you got time to research random crap on the internet."

Dexter peeked behind the TV. "What do you make of this set up?"

John leaned over the dresser to see the hookups in the back. "Standard internet and Ethernet set up. But why would they use a Russian internet company in LA? I'm sure that costs a fortune. Is that even legal?"

"We're in a Russian hotel. I don't think these guys are reflecting on the place of law in our land."

"True. But it must cost a fortune to run internet over here from Russia. With all the options in the states for internet, why spend all the money on Russian technology?"

"More money than we got. We know the address is local. The company is right in our backyard. That must mean something, right?"

John took another look at the back of the TV. "The set-up is odd. It has the internet. But there's a second connection for a satellite. It's hard to know if the Russian channel is being fed by the internet or satellite, or both?"

"You think Russian propaganda is being sent somewhere else through a satellite?"

"Anything is possible," John said, scrunching his face after bending over.

"I took down the address of the company. Not a bad idea to check out this place and see what's going on. Not much else to go on right now."

22

A short Russian with a lisp questioned Dexter and John in the hotel lobby. He'd wondered the progress they'd made on finding Pope's father and Boris. In a firm and yet awkward threat like he'd not do what he promised, the Russian told the boys to focus on the mission, or else. Dexter thought he could drop the small Russian with a blow to the neck.

He refrained.

Dexter and John lied about being close to finding Boris and Pope's dad and wanted to check out the internet company instead. They believed something in this place would unlock the mysteries with the movie studio and lead to finding Boris and Pope's dad. Dexter didn't care all that much about the missing criminals and felt obligated to protect these girls at the movie studio. Pope's mom still stuck in his mind. Rescuing dad would help her cause and he hated seeing her suffer. But in Dexter's mind everyone involved seemed untrustworthy, and he was feeling indifferent to the entire mission.

The lispy Russian let the boys take the Prius on their

adventure and didn't ask many questions. Dexter flipped John the keys and let him drive for a change. It tired him, dodging the millions of cars on the road. Let John stress out for a while.

John jammed a lever in front of the driver seat and pushed the padded seat almost into the back seats. His long and meaty legs needed more space. "Is this car built for children? Sure as hell ain't built for a grown ass men."

"You're not a typical man. A man and a half," Dexter said, strapping his seat belt.

"Funny, Dex. You're in a mood this morning. You talk with Samantha yet?"

Dexter aimed the air conditioner vent toward his face as the day was already warm for ten AM. "Nope. Just tired of this place. I feel like the walls are closing in on me. You can't escape the people and busyness. How does anyone live here with no open spaces? I want to get home and leave LA behind."

Dexter punched in the Russian internet company. "Take a right onto the highway. I think the company is near downtown."

"Nope. Runet is next to Skid Row."

"The band?"

"No, country boy. I did research last night. Skid Row is an area in LA with a massive homeless population. Not safe after dark. I found it interesting this company was in one of the rougher areas. Cheap rent?"

Dexter shrugged as he reflected on the location of the company. He scrolled over the map on his phone and zoomed in close. "Impressive, John. You did some homework on a case. The BBQ last night inspire you to chase bad guys?"

John hit the blinkers and eased onto the highway.

"Dreams about swimming in pools of Diet Cherry Coke did the trick."

"You need to ease up on the sugar water."

John shook his head. "Sugar free. What's the play when we get to Runet?"

"We play it straight. No costumes or man-buns," Dexter said, slapping John on his flabby arm. "We act like tourists interested in business and technology. No funny stuff. We'll ask for a tour and see what Runet is all about."

"What if they don't do tours?"

"We'll worry about Plan B later."

The boys took the twenty minute drive to Runet and pulled into a parking spot on the street. The building was an unassuming warehouse that blended into the rundown neighborhood. Lots of large windows on the front and a nice glass door entry. If they were trying to hide something, they weren't trying very hard. Dexter told John to not screw things up as they exited the Prius.

A Hispanic guy pushing a shopping cart came up behind the boys and asked for some change. Dexter tossed him a dollar bill, and the man said God bless. Dexter and John weren't used to seeing this many homeless people in one place. Small town LeClaire didn't have many homeless, unless you counted the occasional house fire that put someone on the street for a night. But family or the church would take care of them.

John watched the homeless guy make his way down the dirty street. Piles of trash swirled around the car, sidewalk, and in the street as the wind kicked up. "They say five thousand people call Skid Row home," John said.

"Anything else you want to tell me Mr. Jeopardy? Sheesh, you're full of facts today."

"It's not that impressive. Wikipedia."

Dexter opened the glass door of Runet and waved John inside the sterile lobby. A wide, Ikea looking, modern desk sat perched in the middle of the room. A good-looking blonde girl about mid-twenties greeted the men. "Hello, and welcome to Runet. How can I help you?"

Deter glanced at John and back at the pretty girl. "Yes, hello. We're from out of town. We love what your company is doing and wondered if you do tours."

The woman gave a puzzled look. "You want a tour of an internet company?" she said, giving John a look over - he was wearing tight athletic pants and an Antique Adventures tee shirt.

Dexter said, "We're from a small town in another state. Not a lot of cutting edge technology companies in the sticks. We run a business and thought it would be fun to see how the sausage is made. Your company's supposed to be one of the best in the country."

"Sausage, sir?" she asked.

"Sorry about the metaphor. Country-speak. Love to see how things work around here. Get some ideas for our town. It's time we got into the twenty-first century."

She waved off the compliments from Dexter. "We're proud of our product and message to the world."

"What message is that?" John asked.

With no hesitation the girl said in a robotic tone. "To be the fastest and most reliable internet service and share the good news of Runet with the world."

"Good news, huh? Sounds like an important mission," Dexter said, leaning on the counter and giving the receptionist pouty eyes, "So, you think you can help us out, give us a tour? We'd love to hear more about this good news."

The receptionist fell into a trance with Dexter's words and chewed on her fingernail. She snapped out of it. "Let me see what I can do. I'll call someone. It's not everyday someone asks for a tour. You boys seem like nice people."

The girl dialed a phone at her desk and turned her swivel chair around and talked in a hushed tone. Dexter leaned across the desk to hear her conversation. "I have a couple gentlemen wanting a tour of the company. Is that allowed? Who do I talk to?"

There was a pause in their conversation. She glanced over her shoulder as Dexter pretended to not be eavesdropping. John wandered around the lobby filled with white leather couches.

She finished the conversation. "Okay, I'll call him," the girl said, then turning back to Dexter, "I need to call one more person and thank you for your patience."

Dexter tipped his John Deere hat.

She dialed the phone again and chatted with someone for a minute. "Mr. Polian will be down soon."

Dexter let the name ring in his mind for a second. He'd expected more of Russian name but didn't dwell on it too long. "Mr. Polian is one of our head officers in the company. He'll take care of you and give you a tour."

The receptionist gave Dexter a second look as he walked away.

John and Dexter relaxed on the white leather couches and waited for Polian. A middle aged man in a sharp blue suit and sandals greeted both boys with a smile and firm handshake.

The face of Polian registered in Dexter's mind, but it wasn't an exact match. He let the thought go.

"You the boys looking for the one dollar tour?"

"It costs money? We're happy to pay," John blurted out.

"Just an expression, kid."

"Thanks for meeting us. We're from out of town and

wanted to learn more about your company. We're business owners in the Midwest. Heard you're the best in the industry."

"You in technology?"

"No, sir, antiques," Dexter said.

"That sounds interesting," Polian said.

"Every day is an adventure."

Polian observed the men and put on a plastic smile. "Not sure if anyone has ever requested a tour. Why do a couple of antique dealers care about an internet company?"

"Kind of a side hobby. Our technology is so bad in our town, we could use a few tips from the best."

"Sure... nothing to hide," he said, in a nervous tone.

Dexter and John thought the comment out of place.

"Let's start in the back where our IT support works to keep the machine running like a top."

Dexter and John followed Polian past the receptionist's desk. The pretty blonde gave Dexter a wink which he enjoyed, despite being married. Sometimes you have to remember you're not dead and that some people still find you attractive.

Dexter tried to start up some small talk. "Polian... Is that Polish? You from LA?"

"German. Have lived in LA my entire life. Raised a couple kids and call this crazy place home."

"Anyone ever say you have a familiar face? I feel like I've seen you before. But this is my first visit to LA so it's unlikely."

"All the time. Must mean I have a boring face."

Polian waved the boys down a long hallway with offices on each side. He explained that many of the managers worked in these offices. They took a hard right out into an open space with hundreds of cubicles. Men and women wore headsets and the chatter in the room created a low rumble.

"Who are these people?" John asked.

"IT and call support. They keep the machine running from the back end. If anyone has a problem with their service these are the men and women to solve all your problems. They also do sales."

Dexter and John weren't that interested in this part of the company. It seemed Runet was just another typical internet company. "Can anyone buy your internet services? Like a couple business owners from Missouri?" Dexter asked.

"Not anyone. We have very select customers. Did you say Missouri? My son was in Missouri last year for work."

"What does he do for work?" John asked.

"Law enforcement."

Polian's familiar features were coming into focus for Dexter. He'd seen the image in his mind before, but where?

"Did your son work for LAPD at some point?" Dexter asked.

"He did. They shipped him off to Missouri for a case. He never said why, but he was helping a small outfit in LeClaire, I think."

John glanced at Dexter and they knew this was either the biggest coincidence in the world's history, or Polian was Jake's dad.

"What's your son's name?" Dexter asked, giving John a smirk.

"Jake. We're not on good terms right now."

Dexter drew his pistol and stuck it between the glasses of Polian. John did the same.

"We know who you are. Why is your name Polian and not Pope? What the hell is going on here?"

Polian raised his hands in surrender and his face turned white. "What are you talking about? I'm telling the truth, my name is Jim Polian. How do you know Jake?"

"Doesn't matter. Why does Jake have the name Pope? Explain..."

"When things got shitty in our relationship, he took his mother's maiden name. He said he wanted nothing to do with me. How do you know my son? Is he okay?"

"We don't know. Jake came to LeClaire to help on a case. He did some shady things and was kicked off the force. You didn't know? How do I know you're his dad?"

Polian's face scrunched up with confusion. "So wait. Why in the hell are two country boys from LeClaire here in LA? Have you seen Jake?"

"Yes, it's a long story. I'm here to rescue you."

"Rescue me? From what? As you can see, I'm fine. I work at Runet and drive a Tesla. I have a girlfriend and live in Manhattan Beach. Is this a joke?"

Polian nodded to the boys and told them to follow him to a back office. He kept his hands up and the boys kept their guns trained on his head.

He opened the office door. "Let me explain."

23

Polian panicked in the sterile office. He tapped the desk and scanned the space like he was looking for his keys. Told the boys not to say anything for fear of being bugged by the Russians.

He opened the door and peeked down the hallway.

No other employees were mingling.

All clear.

Polian slinked back into the office and stood on a chair, and unplugged a camera mounted in the ceiling's corner.

"Things make little sense. It'll be clear in a moment. We only have a few minutes before they get suspicious."

Dexter trained the gun on Polian as he paced the office and was scratching the armpits of his blue suit.

"Who are *they*?" Dexter asked.

"The Russians."

"What Russians?"

"The Russians who forced me to work in this terrible place."

"What is this place? Isn't it an internet company?"

"Not the half of it."

"Why should I believe you? From the minute I stepped off the plane in LA everyone has been lying their asses off. Jake Pope is caught up in some shit and lying through his teeth. Give me a reason..."

Polian was getting animated and talking with his hands. "Everything I said is true. Jake is my son. I screwed up and wasn't a good dad. His mom divorced me years ago. After the divorce he wanted nothing to do with me. Blamed me for everything."

"He didn't mention that part. Said you were still married. Why should I believe you?"

"You don't have to. But Jake likes to tell that story. When he was younger, it felt better to pretend his family was still together. School counselors said it was some kind of coping mechanism."

"Why do you work here? Jake said you owned a gym, and did sales back in the day."

"Because my life's one failure after another. I racked up some gambling debts with a Russian bookie. I bought a business and tried to use it to pay off the debts. It didn't work like I'd hoped; I made some money, but not enough to pay off the bookies. The Russians took over the business and now they own my ass. I'm at their mercy and whatever they want, I do."

Dexter placed the gun back in his jeans and John kept his trained on Polian, just in case this was all a game. "Wait, they have you working at a Russian internet company? Why?" Dexter asked.

"Work off my debts. I'm business savvy and worked in technology sales for years. They thought I could be useful while they take over the world."

"Take over the world? What do you mean?" John asked.

Polian whispered. "I don't know everything that goes on

at Runet. But it's a front for some evil takeover. They're trying to brainwash these young girls into taking their message to the world. And Jake's part of it."

"Yes, he is. That's why I'm supposed to rescue you. The Russians are holding us hostage and telling us if we don't find you and some dude named Boris they'll kill our families. But at least they promised to pay."

"Boris Popov? If so, I wouldn't count on any payday. He's a sick dude."

"You know him?"

Polian shook his head and slumped into the chair. He sighed. "Popov is the bookie I owe money. I invested in a gym. After the Russians took over I found out they were laundering money. I did their accounting and didn't want my name on things. I threatened to go to the police. They were trying to throw me under the bus and make me the fall guy. If I said anything they'd kill me and all my relatives."

"Sounds familiar," Dexter said.

"Damn, these guys," John said.

"Well, if you're alive, it solves part of our mission. Where's Boris?" Dexter asked.

"I don't know. But you don't want to mess with that Russian. He's running the whole operation and not a guy you want on your bad side."

"Why did Jake say Boris was missing? What's the point of pretending you and Boris were kidnapped?"

Polian caressed his chin and thought for a second. "Why would Jake lie? I'd never work with Boris in a million years, I'd rather die."

"You're working for him now. Why should we believe you?"

"I'm nothing in the organization. They're just using me to run their internet business and pay back the money I owe. Make an example out of me for the rest of the cult. I might have done some stupid things in my life, but I'm not buddying up with a bunch of psychotic Russians. I do have an ounce of integrity left."

"Did you say cult?"

"Maybe not in a technical sense. But the Russians are trying to brainwash these young girls and spread their message. It's cult-like," Polian said, giving air quotes.

John and Dexter took in the new information and their brains were about to explode. Dexter wanted a work-vacation to make a few bucks. Let the fires at home cool down. But now he was in deep. Dexter wanted out in the worst way.

In a sudden burst of inspiration Polian opened the door and waved the boys into the hallway. He didn't seem to care that the Russians might come and find him any minute. "Follow me. I want to show you the lengths these Russians will go to to spread their message."

Dexter and John hesitated and gave into his plea. The hallway was empty as the employees left for lunch. Polian moved with caution and scanned each office as they worked their way to the back doors of the warehouse.

A long alley behind the warehouse led the men out to a busy street. Polian glanced back. "I want you to meet some people."

Polian hung a left, and then another quick left, and darted down a second alley. About a dozen Coleman camping tents in a variety of colors lined the alley. Polian waved the boys to a blue tent with the doors closed. "Sylvia, you in there?"

The sound of a quick rip of a zipper and a young lady in her twenties with dreadlocks opened the makeshift home. Dexter and John were not comfortable with the ramshackle living quarters and the smells coming from the woman and the streets of Skid Row. A foreign world to the boys from LeClaire.

"I want you to meet someone," Polian said.

The woman looked the boys up and down and smiled. "They're not from around here."

"Perceptive, they aren't. From Missouri," Polian said, with a gentle smile.

"I've been there. Family vacation when I was a kid. Where is that place with the trains? Union Station?"

Dexter was impressed with her knowledge of the show-me-state. "Union Station is in Kansas City. One of the oldest train stations in America."

"You gotta be known for something I guess," the woman said.

Polian guided the conversation back to the reason he took the boys to the alley. "Tell these tourists how you ended up on the streets?"

"Runet."

"The Russian internet company?" John asked.

The woman laughed and shook her head. "If you'd like to believe that. They take the dreams of young and talented performers and flush them down the sewers of LA. Promise fame and fortune. But it's all a front for world domination."

Polian waved Sylvia to say more. "I was part of their young stars program. They would find young actresses to intern at their company and promise to get them on TV or in movies. Well, that was a bunch of shit. These girls have no idea what they signed up for."

Dexter asked, "Why would girls intern at an internet company? Isn't that what the Odessa Film Studio is for? What's the point?"

"Oh, you know more than most. The internet company

is a modern version of slave labor. They give these young girls low-paying jobs at Runet during the day, and promise to give them screen time at Odessa in the evening. But it's a bunch of bullshit," Sylvia said, staring at the ground.

"How so?" John asked.

"If you question anything you end up on the street like me. And the others," Sylvia said, pointing to the other tents lining the alley. Two girls from a red tent poked their heads out and were watching the conversation in the dirty alley.

"How'd you end up on the street?" Dexter asked, glancing at Polian, who was nodding for Sylvia to share more.

"Fell into the trap and agreed to intern with Runet for screen time. I lived in LA for a couple years and was getting nowhere in my career. Moved from Baton Rouge and tried to make it in Hollywood. A guy approached me one day at the gym and told me I had the look. He gave me his card, and well, the rest is history as they say."

"Who was the guy?"

A tear welled up in Sylvia's eye. She wiped it clear and smudged dirt on her tan skin. "Jake Pope. He promised me a career... and I bit."

Dexter said under his breath, *damn that guy*. "You sure it was Jake Pope?"

She nodded. "When he wanted me to do things I was uncomfortable with I told the higher ups. Which doesn't work when Jake's one of them."

"You mind me asking what he did?" Dexter asked in a gentle tone.

"No problem. He wanted to hook up. I always told myself I'd earn my way in Hollywood with no shortcuts. Too many actors sell out for a chance on a movie or TV show. Sleep with anyone and everyone. I wouldn't do it. He kept pressuring me and telling me I'd ruin my career if I refused his advances. I guess he wasn't joking as I live here now," Sylvia said, tapping the side of the tent with her running shoe.

John chimed into the conversation. "Why didn't you tell the police?"

Polian laughed. "If only it was that easy. The Russians are in bed with LAPD. Little people like us have no leverage."

Sylvia pointed to the rows of tents on the streets. "You think it's an accident Runet is located near Skid Row? Play with the mother bee and you get stung. Anyone who questions the powerful Russians is black-balled and sent to the streets. Finding work is impossible," Sylvia said, with a sigh.

Polian thanked Sylvia for her time and the other ladies who were watching the conversation. Dexter and John wished them the best, and they walked back toward Runet.

Polian pulled the boys next to a building a block down from Runet. "I could've got myself killed today. Still a possibility. The Russians could be watching. But you heard my dilemma from Sylvia, right? My son's not a good person. Jake's ruining lives. Someone must stop him."

"How'd you meet Sylvia? You obviously know each other."

"I was walking back from lunch one day. She told me about how she ended up in the streets. We both knew we could get ourselves killed for having a conversation. We had to do something. Life is too short and I'm done living under the thumb of the Russians. I screwed up and made a mess of most relationships in my life," Polian said, pausing, and then shaking his head and kicking the curb. "I'm afraid I wounded the soul of Jake. That's why he's living such a reckless life. Never thought it would come to putting away your only son."

Dexter reached out a hand and grasped the shoulder of Polian. "I have three kids of my own. The sins of the father are real. But I believe in grace too. Not everything is your fault. Your son has to take responsibility for his actions. No matter what you did, nothing gives him the right to hurt innocent girls."

Polian nodded and appeared to find solace in the words of Dexter. John wandered the sidewalk watching the two men share their stories. "You guys done? I'm getting hungry," John said.

Dexter waved him off. "One second, fatty."

Polian found a smile in the moment of pain. "You guys have a good thing going. It's important to have close friends."

"Most days it works," Dexter said, trying to find the next words. "I don't know if this is helpful, or not. But we're willing to help you stop Pope and the Russians."

Polian held up his hands. "I don't think a couple of country boys from Missouri want to get mixed up in this shit storm. Thanks for the offer, but I'll fly solo."

"You're forgetting a small detail. I'm here to rescue you, remember? We're all in the same shit storm. Except the Russians don't know we'll take them down from the inside. Beat them at their own game. They want to use us, we'll use them."

John wandered over and asked when they could eat. "We have a new partner for taking down some Russians," Dexter said, slapping John on the arm.

"Cool, but let's eat first, I'm no good for anyone with an empty stomach," John said.

24

Polian went back to Runet and played it cool. He finished up his day and was planning on meeting the guys later in the evening, if they could sneak away from the hotel.

Dexter was working on a new plan, knowing Polian was alive and well and not named Pope. With Polian on board he was confident he'd be the missing ingredient for taking down Pope and the Russians.

Dexter gunned the Prius down Sunset Boulevard. "You trust him?" Dexter asked John, who was watching cars fly by.

"Who?"

"Polian."

"Another reason being a dad scares the hell out of me. The potential of ruining your kids and turning them into monsters seems high. Good luck with that," John said, sipping a Coke.

"You sure get honest after a full stomach. Thanks for the vote of confidence. You think my kids have a chance of not becoming monsters?"

"Well, let's look at the facts. A dad who's on his second marriage. First marriage ended in horrendous circumstances. Wife and child die in an accident, rest in peace Lisa and Jack," John said, pointing to the sky, "The dad now dealing with a second wife and three kids always wondering if they're replacements of the first. The dad runs a successful antique business and side business, but is always gone. Choosing work over family. Yeah, the kids will be fine," John said with a thumbs up.

"Thanks Dr. Phil. I happen to enjoy my work. Sorry if you and my family don't see it that way."

John raised his hands. "No judgment. I'm a single dude living with his mom. You wanted the truth, and you go it."

"Let's get back to the task at hand. We don't typically work with other teammates. But we have to trust Polian. Or this won't work. He's essential for taking down these bastards," Dexter said.

"So, if Pope wanted us to find Polian, and Polian is working for the Russians, and now is safe and sound, what's really going on here? Is Pope working another angle?" John asked.

"That's what I've been thinking. Boris is still out in the wild and like I said, we need to cut off the head of the snake. He seems to be spraying venom all over LA. But why would Pope lie about his dad?"

"My only thought is Pope is clueless about his dad. No idea he's working at Runet. Maybe there're different factions within the organization. Pope's lower rung and out of the loop. He's just a distraction to keep away from the big boys. Pope isn't Russian blood, making for loyalty issues. Runet and the studio are different animals? Not connected. You think someone is going rogue within the organization?"

Dexter steered the Prius off the highway and headed to

the hotel only ten minutes out. The traffic was thick as usual and the air was mild, which was typical.

"Pope told us to find Polian and Boris. That's our way out. They don't know we found a clue at Runet. We got a lucky break in finding Polian. You think they wanted us to find him? Why have us chase down a guy that already works for them? Maybe your theory is right. Someone knows Polian is working for Runet, and they're working something in the shadows."

"Come on, Dex. The chances of you finding the Runet logo on the back of the TV, driving to the address, and finding Polian, is not what the Russians were banking on. They could've done something simpler," John said.

Dexter doubted his confidence in Polian. Could they trust his story? Was he rogue? Dexter sat with his thoughts for another moment. He remembered Sylvia and the tears in her eyes. She was an actress, and they pay actresses to pretend. But her story was convincing. Could Polian and Sylvia have worked up a story trying to trap the boys?

"We can't go off theory and hunches. We work with facts. Polian's working off debts at Runet. He's at odds with Pope and knows he's dirty. As do we. Pope sent us to find Polian and Boris for money and freedom. Polian's alive and well. Boris is still on the loose. We learned from Sylvia that Runet and Odessa Studios are taking in girls promising fame, and that it appears to be a front for something else. The something else is not clear, yet. How do all these streams flow into one river?" Dexter asked, staring off through the windshield into the noisy streets of LA.

"Why don't we drop some bait in the water?" John asked.

"No time for fishing, fatty."

"No, we tell the Russians we found Polian. See how they react?"

"I don't want to get Polian in trouble. He's important for us taking down these dudes."

"You don't understand. Like I said before. If the organization is a mess, and someone is going rogue, no one will care we found Polian. But if this is legit, and Pope isn't lying for once, we tell them we found Polian, and we lead them into a trap. If they want Polian, they go through us. Except we lead them into the bee hive," John said.

Dexter liked the initial idea but wanted to make sure Polian wasn't in unnecessary danger. "I like it. But let's play it cool at the hotel and wait to discuss with Polian later tonight. We set up a meeting at Denny's. I got another idea."

The Prius rolled into the Odessa Hotel. Dexter and John talked through their next move. John was fine with the idea and trusted Dexter more than a brother.

They walked through the sterile lobby and no Russians were in sight. The boys took the elevator to their room and relaxed and changed clothes. Whenever they went back to their room someone always called to check in on them. Dexter waited for the call.

The phone rang.

"Any more progress?" the Russian voice asked.

"Maybe."

"Time is running short. If you don't find these guys the deal's off. And things go bad for the country boys."

"Easy, friend. We're doing our best. I happened to find something interesting today. The internet went out in the room. I found the company and made a call. Everything should be good now. Can't do much without internet, right?"

There was silence on the line for fifteen seconds. The Russian came back on the line. "You stay focused on the mission. We can handle things like the internet, you understand?" he said, in a firm tone.

"You seem upset over something so silly. We were just trying to help out. The days get long without the internet. I know for your business the internet is vital for your message, am I right?"

Two quick thumps on the door startled John, who was watching Dexter do his magic on the phone.

Dexter told the man to hold.

Two wide shouldered Russians with stern looks on their faces stood in the doorway.

"Please come with us."

25

Two Russians led Dexter and John to a conference room in the back of the hotel. They asked the boys to find a seat at a long round table surrounded by a dozen chairs. A man larger than John said someone would be with them shortly.

Dexter's stomach rumbled, and he wondered if they had been watching them at Runet. Had they seen them interact with Polian? John glanced over at Dexter and gave a shrug ,and seemed to be calm about the situation.

The door opened and two different men entered the room. Jazz music played in the background from the speakers in the ceiling. Jake Pope settled into an office chair at the opposite end of the table and what appeared to be his bodyguard stood to the right. Pope sipped on a Starbucks.

"Good to see you fellas again. Sounds like you've been busy."

Dexter glanced at John and back to Pope. "Yeah, just trying to find your dad and Boris. Like you told us. So we can leave this hell hole behind."

Dexter was holding everything back to not jump over

the long conference table and choke out Pope. He hated the smug look on his face and laid back attitude, knowing what he had done to those girls.

Pope sipped on the coffee. "How's the mission going? Any leads?"

Dexter didn't appreciate Pope's nonchalant questioning. "Nothing worth pursuing," Dexter said, with a crooked smile, "The hardest part of working a case in LA is the traffic. It takes forever to get anywhere. You talk to someone and it takes hours to get back. How do you do it?"

"It grows on you. Anyone in particular you've been talking to?"

"A girl who used to hang around the gym where Boris worked. Dead end. Still searching for something solid to find your people. It won't be long."

"Did you plan on mentioning your little visit to my mother.... Why you would do such a thing? She has nothing to do with the mission, and she's sick," Pope said, taking another sip of coffee.

"When you don't know people in a strange city you start with the familiar. Doesn't it make sense to talk to the person who's closest to the missing person?"

Pope placed his coffee on the table. He rose from his chair and rubbed his hands through his flowing blonde hair. "Yes, it makes sense, country boy. But my mom has no relationship with my father. He's an asshole who deserves to die for the shit he's done to our family. You already know, and you heard it from my mother's own mouth. Leave her out of this and stick to the plan," Pope said, his face now turning red.

"What plan are you talking about, Pope? There's no plan. You fly me out here and make up some damn story about a case you can't solve. I take the bait and now you want me to find your estranged father and some Russian mobster? You send my partner to help and threaten me and our families. Promising money and a trip home. What plan? Why should I listen to another damn word you say, you're a liar, and a sad excuse of a human. Why shouldn't I put a bullet in your skull right now?"

Dexter had no intention of getting so fired up with Pope. But the rage boiling inside was too much to handle. He thought about Samantha and the kids and his true mission to get back home and try to mend the fences of their relationship. He couldn't care less about Pope right now.

Pope paced the conference room and the bodyguard watched the two men going at it. Pope slid a gun from his jeans waistband and waved it at Dexter and John. "I'd be careful with your tone Dexter. I'm the one holding the cards, and I have a straight flush. The hand you're holding is a pair of twos, and everyone knows you should fold. I'm not a dummy, Dex. We've been watching you. And it sounds like you have been meeting with more people than you're willing to admit. You care to share?"

Dexter's hand brushed the pistol jammed in the back of his Wrangler's. He so wanted to yank it out and put a hole in Pope's head. Dexter had to face the music. "So what? What if I haven't shared every move we've made? There's no plan, remember? You didn't tell me what I could and couldn't do. Who I could talk to, or not. I live by my own script and work the way I want. You should understand that Private I. If you don't like the way I do things, find someone else."

Pope strolled across the conference room and cozied up next to Dexter. His face was no longer red, and a calm washed over him. He switched to a gentle whisper. "I saw you. This was not part of the plan. Those whores are nothing but useless trash. They don't have the talent to make it in our business. Whatever they told you is lies. And liars end up living on the streets and never see their name in lights."

Dexter and John could feel the chill in the air from Pope's cold demeanor. "I got it. They pay actors to play make believe. Maybe those girls are liars. You're pretty good at acting too, what does that make you?" Dexter asked.

Pope jammed the end of the gun into Dexter's neck and took a deep breath. He somehow stayed calm. "You have no idea the shit I've gone through to get where I am. Don't think some dirty whores, or my father, will take all of this away from me."

"Is your father a liar too? We had a nice chat, and if he's anything like you, he can't be trusted."

Pope backed up like he'd been stung by a bee and was now prancing around the room and grabbing at his hair and waving the gun. "Damn it, Dexter. You know how I feel about my father. He's a dirty man who doesn't deserve to live. If it was up to me, he'd have been erased from the planet long ago. Right now, I don't have that kind of power."

Dexter thought about John's theory of the Russian organization having factions. He wondered if someone was holding Pope back from doing something to his dad. Was Pope a puppet and controlled by a higher up?

"Aren't you the King Snake, running things around here, Pope? Sounds like someone else is controlling you like a puppet. Holding you back from being the big cheese. Is it Boris? Putin? Since we know your dad isn't missing. Anything you want to share with us?" Dexter said, with extra snark.

Pope pinned the gun against his own head and continued to pace the small conference room. "I have no idea how you found my father and don't give a shit. And

Boris can go to hell, for all I care. He's just a suave Russian who uses his good looks to prey on woman and take advantage for his own gain. He stumbled into fame and fortune by accident because of his Russian connections in LA."

"You sound bitter about it," John said.

"Pipe down Shrek. No one gives a shit. I'm no Boris. He's the problem with our organization. If it were up to me, things would be different."

Dexter had seen the insecurities of Pope from the moment he met him last year in LeClaire. He wanted to press the knife in deeper. "From what I can tell this is the story of your life. Dad was absent, never said he loved you. You work a prestigious job. A job you hate but do it anyway, trying to make daddy take notice of you. Things go south and you're looking for significance and maybe control. You find it here, whatever this place is. Now things aren't going as you hoped. A sad life, Pope, and just like these girls trying to make it in Hollywood, you're no different. Remember, it's the selfie generation, everyone wants to be famous in their own way. Someone told me that once."

Pope paused at the foot of the long conference table and placed his gun on the surface. He hung his head and stared at the table. Pope then gently lifted his head with his face now beet red. "You nailed me, Dex. I'm just an insecure kid from So Cal dealing with daddy issues. Just like the millions of girls who come from small towns searching for fame. But everyone knows it's not about fame. It's about fixing something inside us. Something in our souls that never seem to be content. No amount of money or power or women ever does the trick. You know that, I know that."

"Poetic, Pope. At least you're honest. So what's the end game here? You become just another statistic? A statistic in the prison system, or a statistic as another unnecessary death because power and fame corrupted a guy with a lot of God-given talents?"

"Not good odds. But I'd rather live on the edge, push all my chips to the middle, and not live an ordinary existence... like my father. What did it get him?"

"Those daddy issues are strong," John said.

Pope ignored the comment from John. He pointed at the bodyguard who had come into the conference room with him, and the other two. Pope dismissed them.

Dexter wondered why Pope would allow himself to be exposed, given the moment. He had to know Dexter and John were armed and could change their minds about Pope and put him down in a second. Why take the risk?

Pope ushered the last Russian out of the room. He bolted the door and closed the blinds that draped a window exposing them to a hallway. Pope then pushed a rolling chair to the corner of the room where a camera was mounted. Like his father earlier in the day, he unhooked the camera's power cord, and let it dangle from the ceiling.

Dexter brushed his gun with the back of his hand a second time. Thought about ending Pope as he slid the rolling chair back to the conference table.

"Let's chat off the record. You've passed every test I've thrown at you. Time to get down to business."

"What test? Is this some kind of game?"

Pope got comfortable in a swivel chair at the end of the conference table and folded his hands. "So, you've met my dad. I have to be honest. Never thought a couple of rednecks from Missouri would find him. How did you do it?"

Dexter was confused about the casual nature of the conversation with Pope. Something was not connecting in his brain. Dexter peeked at John who was sharing a similar confused look. "Don't underestimate these rednecks. But technically rednecks were miners from the South, we prefer country."

"I stand corrected."

"Finding your dad was lucky. Lucky is better than good, someone once said. The back of the TV had an address for your internet provider. We looked it up and made a visit. Your dad happened to be working at Runet. I guess the stars aligned for us."

Pope slapped the table. "Damn, Dexter. You do have natural detective talent. That shit doesn't happen to everyone."

Dexter enjoyed the compliment for a moment. "What is this about?"

"My dad was never missing. And Boris isn't gone," Pope switched to a whisper, "This was a test."

"For who?"

"Both of us. The organization is testing me. Seeing if I have the skills to pull off a job. And a test for you guys, to see if I could trust you. It was all made up. You passed with flying colors. Think of it as the scrimmage before the big game."

"Have you been playing us the entire time?" John asked.

"Not the entire time. The job was a test for me to move up the ranks in the organization. I needed someone I trusted to be the guinea pigs. You fit the bill. But I had a different agenda all along."

Dexter threw up his hands. "Wait a minute, asshole. You flew John and I out here to La La Land to mess with us? It was all so you could move up in the Russian mafia? Or whatever the hell this organization is?"

"No, let me finish. I said, I had another agenda. I would work with you boys. But not on the original case. Not everything has been a lie. I have something better I think you'll be excited about. That's why you're here. No way I'd waste your time on your first trip to LA," Pope said, with a smirk.

Dexter stood to his feet. He shook his head and glanced down at John, who was still seated in his chair. "You believe this guy? He thinks after all this, we'd consider another job?" Dexter said, waiting for John to respond.

"I don't know, we're here. Let's hear him out. What's the job, Pope?" John asked.

"Boris. He's a bad dude. That's my other agenda. Trust me, he's the guy you boys would love to see sent away for a long time. He's preying on innocent people," Pope said.

"Trust you? *Trust you*? You've lied from day one. Why in God's green earth would we trust you? You're not a saint, lover boy," Dexter said.

"I know, I know. It all looks confusing and I have a ton of egg on my face. But it's all part of a bigger plan to take down Boris. Let me explain it further tomorrow morning. We don't have time. People will get suspicious."

A voice called out in the hallway. Someone knocked on the conference room door.

Pope slid a card across the table. "Meet me at this address tomorrow morning. It will all make sense, trust me."

The voice got louder in the hallway. "Pope, what's going on in there? Why is the door locked?"

Dexter scanned the card. His head told him not to trust Pope after the buckets of lies. But his heart thought Pope might be telling the truth, and stopping Boris and the Russians might save these girls from a life of ruin. Justice always wins in the end.

Dexter raised a finger at Pope. "We show up tomorrow and you lay it on the table. If we think something is off, we leave and head back to Missouri."

The man in the hallway was shaking the lock and yelling.

Pope stood from the chair and walked to the boys at the end of the table. He knelt down and stared at Dexter. "Boris knows about you. He will kill you if you try to leave. This is not a game. A lot of lives are at stake. Please trust me. I need your help. The only way home is taking out Boris."

Dexter was haunted by the piercing blue eyes of Pope. They looked like he was a lost kid trying to find his mother in a department store. Scared and serious. Dexter wasn't sure how to get out of LA, and it appeared it was at the mercy of Pope.

"Fine. We'll hear you out."

Pope grinned, strolled back to the camera, fastened the cord back into the power supply, and unlocked the door.

He told the body guards to calm down and to escort the boys back to the hotel.

It would be a short night of sleep.

26

Dexter tossed and turned after receiving the offer from Pope. John snored and slept like a baby, which was normal as things tended to not stress him out. Dexter wanted to hear Pope out. Not because he trusted him. Trust was broken long ago. Dexter needed a way out of LA and getting back to his family as priority one.

Dexter would be guarded with every move he made with Pope.

The boys took the Prius to Messenger Coffee, a hipster joint off Sunset Boulevard near China Town. It took thirty minutes to travel ten miles in the thick of morning rush hour traffic. Dexter almost lost his mind when someone cut him off on the highway. Leaving LA couldn't come soon enough.

"How'd you sleep?" Dexter asked John.

"Like a baby, you?"

"What else is new. Not so good. Too much on the brain. After yesterday's bizarre turn of events you still slept like a baby?"

"It's a gift. Try not to sweat the small stuff."

"You aren't small. I wish you'd care a little more about, oh, when a dude's been lying his ass off, holds us hostage, tells us everything has been a sham, and now needs our help. Nothing, no stress...?"

John shrugged.

"Here's the deal. We listen to Pope. I'm not allowing this guy to put us up the river without a paddle. If the job is wonky, we bail."

"We have no other options."

"Why?"

"He said Boris will kill us. Our only ticket home is through Pope."

"Come on, John. No one writes our script. There's always another path to take."

"All right, whatever you say boss."

Dexter pulled into Messenger Coffee. The coffee shop was bustling with dozens of morning commuters getting their jolt of caffeine. John giggled at the amount of man-buns buying coffee and the ones already sitting with their laptops at a variety of small tables in the large space.

"The man-bun is an epidemic in LA," John said, with a smile.

Dexter laughed and ordered a coffee. John ordered a coffee too and scanned the store for Pope. They spotted him in the back typing on a laptop and sipping on a cappuccino.

He rose from his stool at the high top table and gave the boys both a handshake. "I wasn't sure you'd come. Let's get right down to it."

"I hope yesterday didn't scare you away. I meant what I said. Boris is a sick bastard. He must be stopped."

Dexter wasn't appreciating the tone of Pope. He was too cavalier in his conversation. Dexter would not allow him to rope them into something without asking more questions. His BS Meter was high.

"Hold up, Pope. We have a lot of questions before anything moves ahead."

Pope raised his hands from the laptop and smiled. "Oh, yeah. No problem. Go for it Dex, fire away."

"I don't give a shit about Boris. I need things cleared up with you. We've done work behind the scenes and you're not coming out smelling like roses. More like rotting pumpkins after Halloween."

Pope scrunched his face after the metaphor. "That's expected. You guys are solid unofficial detectives," Pope said, with a wink, "What do you want to know, I'm an open book. No more games."

"Barber, ring a bell? He lived next door to Jill Morris."

"Sure does. A former Vietnam vet. Pain in the ass. Always pissed at someone or something. I ran into him a couple times when I'd visit Jill."

"He said you came around Jill's apartment. He heard yelling and fighting the night she died. Is that true?"

"What couple doesn't fight? But I wasn't around when she died. I was working on PI stuff."

"Did you kill her?" Dexter asked in a calm tone sipping his coffee.

Pope raised his hands and glanced at John and back to Dexter. "Come on, boys. You go from bickering with your girlfriend to homicide? Dexter, you were in the room. Someone murdered Jill. But I didn't do it, man. We dated for five minutes. Just a fling. Did Barber say I killed her?"

"In not so many words. But he also mentioned someone else coming by the apartment. A Russian? Could Boris have been sleeping with Jill?"

Pope paused, sipped his coffee, and gave a blank stare.

"My guess would be, yes. He was banging every girl in the organization. Jill was a good girl, but easily persuaded."

"Is that why you preyed on her? Easy notch in your belt."

"What the hell Dexter? You're making a lot of assumptions. I told you... we had fun, a few trips, and that was it. I'm a lot of things, but a murderer is not one. Boris kill her?"

"Barber said he heard yelling and screaming the night they killed her. Someone was in the apartment with her. Which rules out suicide. It could've been you, or Boris. No more games, or we leave."

"Why would I have any reason to kill Jill? She was just a young girl trying to find a career in LA. I ain't no murderer fellas."

"Given your track record why should I believe anything you say, ever?"

"I lied for another reason. There's something else going on I need help with. Trust me. Jill's death is puzzling," Pope said, his eyes growing larger with intensity.

"Hold on... I'm not done. Tell me about your mother. Does she have cancer?" Dexter asked.

Pope grinned. "Dexter, come on, bro. You saw her in the assisted living place. We went to the hospital when she fainted. My mother isn't doing well. I saw her yesterday."

"You said the bills were tight. Payed with your private investigation business money. But because your dad was missing the bills were piling up. Now you apparently work with the Russians and don't seem to hurt for cash. True or false?"

"I'm impressed, Dexter, with your attention to detail. True and false. True, my dad was paying the bills. True, I do have a private investigation business that doesn't pay much. False, some things changed in my financial portfolio. I do have some cash."

"Explain."

"My dad was in a tight spot. He bought the gym and was trying to pay off his gambling debts. All the while trying to pay mom's bills. When he found out about the Russians laundering money through the business, and he spoke up, they put him into their debt. He got the job at Runet as penance. But something else happened along the way."

"What's that?"

"A story broke about Goldie's Gym being under investigation for money laundering and ties to the Russian mafia. My relationship with Dad was nonexistent. I snooped around to see what I could find on Dad and the Russians. Well, one thing led to another, and they offered me a job. A job to keep my mouth shut about everything."

"Did you find something?"

"Yes, and because I had connections with LAPD, I told them I could take them down."

"Why didn't you?"

"They offered me money, a lot of money. I was thinking about mom. I could pay her bills, save a struggling business, and then get out. I was a desperate man. Desperate times call for desperate measures. You've been there, Dex. After Lisa and your son died, and Antique Adventures was tanking, you took the side hustle to stop a killer. You would've done the same thing, right? We do crazy shit for the people we love," Pope said, with eyes turning red.

"Every situation is unique. So, you went to the dark side? How'd you think this would end? One day, you'd say, hey, I'm done now. These Russians don't seem like the accommodating type."

"Mom was a first priority. I wasn't thinking straight. Now I've seen enough, and it's time to take them down."

"Helping your mom is a noble thing. Jumping in bed with the Russian mafia is not. I have a few more questions."

"What about Sylvia? She lives on the streets in Skid Row. She said you made passes at her and she rejected them. Now she lives in a tent because you black balled her from making a go at being an actress. True?"

Pope sipped the last drops of his coffee which was now cold. "It looks bad. I made a pass at her, but she was flirty too. I didn't black ball her; I don't have that kind of power in the organization. That was all Boris' doing. Trust me."

"Why would you ruin these girls' lives?"

"That's why I asked you to help me. I've had enough. I can't be part of this any longer. The money is great, but I can't play the game. I'm not that kind of guy."

"Money corrupts. How do we know you're not leading us into the belly of the beast?"

"The job was harmless at first. They asked me to recruit. Find actors to work at Runet and Odessa. It paid a lot of money, like I said. I'm no saint and manipulated some girls to recruit them into the organization. Thought I could justify the money and working in the organization to help mom. I can't any more..." Pope said, and now a small tear was welling up in his eye.

"I can't change the past and don't expect you to trust me. I have to earn it back. But I saw you guys work in LeClaire. Most guys on the force would be jealous of your skills. And you do it for the right reasons. Someone must hold bad people accountable. I want those kinds of guys on my team. The Russians need accountability for what they've done to these girls," Pope said.

Dexter wanted to walk away and never see Pope again. He didn't know how John felt at the moment but Pope was telling a convincing story. Something in his voice gave a sense in Dexter's gut they could trust him, at least for now. Dexter thought back to Sylvia in the streets and wanted no part in seeing girls abused by the Russians any longer.

"I want to believe you Pope, I do. But you've put us through hell in LA. You've lied and broken trust. Where I come from trust is everything. When it's broken, it's hard to mend. But I also come from a people that believe in grace. When trust is broken, sometimes you have to forgive and give a person a second chance."

Pope glanced at John and back at Dexter. "Are you saying you're in? Will you help me stop the Russians?"

John would go along with Dexter no matter what he decided. That's how their relationship had worked since birth. John trusted Dexter and most of the time everything worked out, even if things took an unconventional path.

"We're in. But under two conditions. You stop lying. And you're paying for our flights homes after we take down these bastards."

Pope gave John and Dexter fist bumps and they exited the hipster coffee shop.

27

One step in AA is to make amends with those you've wronged. Pope felt guilty about lying to his mother and the work he'd been doing with the Russians. Money wasn't as tight as he made it sound. Pope came clean and told her what was up, and thought it wise for Dexter and John to attend the meeting and inform Mom about the mission.

Pope had to play it cool with the Russians if they had a chance of finding Boris. For all they knew Dexter and John were still being strung along and in search of Pope's dad and Boris. The boys slept at the hotel and told the Russians they were hunting for the missing criminals. *No luck, hoping for a break soon.*

Pope punched the gas in a black Chevy Tahoe and darted around a group of slower drivers. He tried to exit highway 110 and get on Pacific Coast Highway, or Highway 1, as the locals called it. The boys gripped the handles inside the SUV as they watched Pope gun it around unsuspecting vehicles. "Can you slow it down Pope? I don't want to be in assisted living with your mother," Dexter said, with panic in his voice.

Pope turned down the radio that was blasting Tom Petty's *Last Dance with Mary Jane.* "When I get nervous, I speed. I've been playing the script in my head of what I want to say to Mom."

"You'll do fine. A little more focus on the road so we can celebrate another birthday," Dexter said.

Pope pulled into the guard shack at the Palos Verdes Assisted Living Facility. He waved a hand at the heavyset man in the shack. They exchanged pleasantries, and the guard mentioned that he hadn't seen Pope in a while. Pope blamed it on work.

The boys entered the sterile assisted living building, which always had a hint of urine in the air. They found the elevators and climbed to Room 307. Pope took a deep breath and prepared his speech in his head.

When Pope knocked on the door, he noticed someone had cracked it. He nudged the door open and called for his mother.

Silence.

He thought nothing as his mother had forgotten to latch the door many times. Sometimes her arthritic hands were too weak to lock the deadbolt.

Dexter and John pulled out their pistols just in case of an intruder.

Pope told them to put their guns away.

He called out again.

Nothing.

Pope waved the boys into the living room. A glass coffee table in front of the couch was shattered in a million pieces. And someone had pulled the drawers under the TV stand out, and they lay with the contents spilled onto the carpet.

Dexter and John pulled out their guns again and checked the back bedroom where Pope's mother slept. Someone had turned the room upside down.

"What the hell? Mom!" Pope yelled, sliding the door out onto the balcony.

He closed the slider. A note taped to the glass was tucked behind the curtain. He must've overlooked it. Pope tore off the handwritten note and read it.

The boys ran into the room and told Pope his mother's room was a mess.

"What did you find?" Dexter asked.

"Boris has been here. He knows everything. He's taken Mom."

"Where would that Russian douche be?" John asked, placing his gun back in a holster on his side.

Pope mulled on something, bolted for the door, and entered the hallway. He pranced up and down the hall. "Has anyone seen Mary Pope? Help us!"

Pope called the boys to follow him down to the front desk on the first floor. They took the stairs.

Pope yelled back as they curved down the three flights of stairs. "This place is on lock down. No one comes in or out without security clearance. The front desk has a list of visitors."

A black woman with bright red lipstick gave Pope a smile as he approached the desk. Pope took a second to catch his breath. "Did someone come for Mom today?"

The woman grinned. "No... hello Jake. I haven't seen you around, handsome. How are you?"

"Lala, I don't have time for chit chat. My mother's missing and someone has broken into her apartment."

Lala was the receptionist at the assisted living facility for twenty years. Nobody would get by her desk without her knowledge.

"What honey? Mary is missing? Someone broke into her place? She didn't come through here today. One way out and it's through me."

Pope grabbed the clipboard on the counter. It had all the names of the visitors and each were time stamped. He tapped on the sheet of paper. "Who the hell is Lewis Howes?"

Lala slid the clipboard across the counter. "He must've come while I was on my lunch. Never heard the name."

"You need to call security, now. This is a bad dude. I want the security tapes. See who came here earlier today."

"Sure baby," Lala said, and picked up the phone to call security.

Dexter pulled Pope aside while Lala called security. "You sure you want security involved? We don't know what we're dealing with here. You get security involved, and that leads to the police. You want that?"

Pope agreed.

Lala finished the call and Pope caught her attention. "Don't call the police yet. I need those tapes. I'll handle the police later."

"Our policy won't allow it. If a tenant has been hurt or an apartment broken into, I have to make a police report."

Pope reached for the hand of Lala. "My sweet chocolate pie. Can this be our secret until I see those tapes? It means a lot..." Pope said, giving a sheepish grin, "I'm working a big case and don't want police swarming this place. It involves my father, and it's kind of personal. Please sweetie..."

Lala batted her black eyelashes. "In another life you'd be my bowl of white chocolate. I'd love to help you Jake, but I could get fired."

Dexter walked over and leaned against the counter.

"Lala is it?"

"Yes."

"I'm Detective O'Kane and work with Jake Pope. We're getting close to solving a case. Can you hold off calling the cops? We'll take a peek at the tapes and get back with you. Deal? No one needs to know..."

Something in the tone of Dexter changed Lala's mind. She whispered. "Please don't get me fired. Tell no-one I'm letting you do this."

The heavyset security guard from the parking lot shack came over to the boys. He called them to a back office. Pope sat behind a small desk and watched the tape of cars coming in and out of the facility.

Pope had the guard rewind the tape to 12:34 PM. Same time on the visitor log.

"Go back two to three minutes. How long to get from the parking lot to the desk?"

"About two minutes, depending on parking. And how fast a person walks," the security card said, tapping on the computer and watching the film speed backwards.

Pope said, "Who is that? What time was that?"

"12:30 PM."

"Anyone else come through the shack before or after 12:34?"

"Nope. Just a guy with dark glasses."

"That's the guy. Can you zoom in on his face?"

The security guard tapped again on the computer. "How's that?"

A frozen image of a man wearing dark-rimmed glasses, black beard, and a thin build stared back at them. Pope leaned to get a better look.

"Who the hell is that? I've never seen him before. Why is he visiting my mom?"

Dexter touched the screen. "Is it Boris?"

"Who's Boris? That wasn't the name he gave me," the security guard said.

"Doesn't matter. Could someone else have entered the facility before or after? Did we miss it?"

"It's been a slow day. I'd remember. He was the only guy to come through at lunchtime. You know him?"

"Nope," Pope said.

Pope thanked the security guard for his time. He also thanked Lala and reiterated not to mention anything to the cops until he called again.

Dexter and John and Pope walked to the front of the facility. "Was it Boris?" Dexter asked, scratching his head.

"No. He's using someone to do his dirty work. Or someone is messing with us. But regardless Mom's missing and we need to find her," Pope said, kicking a rose bush at the entrance of the facility.

28

B oris stood behind Mary Pope in the dressing room of the Odessa Studios. She sat calmly in a director's chair as he stared at her in a mirror. They tied Mary's hands to a chair. A young blonde woman applied makeup to her wrinkled and sun blotched skin.

"Jim told me you've always wanted to be a star, Mary. Now's your chance to be on the small screen."

"Go to hell. You know nothing about me, or my family. We've given you everything you asked for, let me go," Mary said, wiggling her frail hands tied to the chair with ropes, and giving out a smoker's cough.

Boris caressed Mary's thin and graying hair, which had been ravished by the cancer treatments. He observed the young woman who wasn't talking and who was focused on applying blush and lipstick on Mary with deft precision. "Russians are a prideful and powerful people. We have steel in our spines. Some say it's because we've endured the harsh winters of our homeland. Others would say our pride comes from being a former world power. One day we'll return to dominance, I'll see to that. Your husband is not a good man.

He tried to derail our message and stop our organization. Now he pays."

"You're delusional. Jim paid off his debts. Why are you doing this? We can get you more money. Please let me go, I'll call my son Jake. He can help."

Boris sneered and wiped the side of Mary's cheek with the back of his hand. "Oh, little Jakey. Our little American boy with aspirations to be part of our powerful organization. Little Jake, like father, like son. He's a traitor just like your husband."

"What are you talking about? Jake doesn't know you. He's a Private Investigator and used to work at LAPD. He doesn't have any idea about Jim working for you."

"Oh, my naïve Mary. If you knew the half of it. Jake would make his sick mother so sad... All the American values you taught your son. Be kind, honest, work hard, and be faithful to one woman. All down the drain. Jake is a bad, bad, boy..."

Mary's eyes welled up in redness as she stared deep into the mirror. She watched Boris' sheepish grin as he played with her hair. "What are you saying? Jake works for you? That isn't possible. I've been to his offices. Jim never mentioned this."

"We're good at pulling wool over the eyes of stupid people. Americans can be so naïve. Jake has a lot to tell you if he ever sees you again. Seems unlikely after the latest stunt he pulled. Broke our code, and I don't like codes being broken," Boris said, pounding his hand on the counter.

The young blonde girl finished applying the makeup on Mary and capped off the lipstick. She glanced up at Boris and gave a forced smile. "Good, Mr. Popov?"

"Yes, my love," Boris said, giving the young woman a soft kiss on her cheek, "Go tell the others to prepare the studio."

The woman scampered out of the dressing room and closed a metal door.

"So is it true you've always wanted to work in Hollywood? You wanted to be the next star in La La Land?"

She nodded. "That was a lifetime ago. Kids got in the way. Sometimes dreams have to die."

Boris rubbed the back of Mary's neck. "Well, today, your dreams will be reborn. Can you read cue cards?"

Mary nodded. A tear trickled down her cheek and made tracks in her freshly applied makeup. "Go to hell. Your message is not what this country stands for. You're a criminal and a womanizer."

Boris stood with his arms akimbo and smiled in the mirror. "Feisty, I like it. You're the kind of girl we'd love to have in our organization. Too bad you're sick and old. Two big problems around here. We need healthy and young women. Consider this contract work. Make it count as this will be your only chance on the small screen. No hard feelings."

Mary ignored the comment. She gave another cough.

Boris yanked a walkie-talkie off his belt and called someone to come into the dressing room. A different blonde woman came over to Mary and fixed the makeup that was now running because of the tears. She asked Boris if everything looked good and he said he was happy with it. He then reiterated that he needed the studio ready before going live.

Boris untied the ropes on Mary's hands and helped her out of the chair.

"Showtime," Boris said, leading Mary out of the dressing room to the news set.

29

P ope and the boys raced out of the assisted living facility. Dexter was convinced that Lala would call the cops and things would go sideways. If the Russians were connected to LAPD things would get messy. Especially since Dexter and John were not official law enforcement. Pope was not exactly on good terms with LAPD. A little digging and they'd see working with the Russians as a huge negative.

The SUV blazed down highway 110 and made a beeline back to Runet. Pope wanted to see if his dad could help track down Boris. Maybe find his mother.

"What's the play?" Dexter asked.

Pope focused on the road and gave blunt and short answers, his face deep in thought. "Runet. See if my dad can help."

John nodded.

"Does Boris have your mom? Why would he do such a thing? She's an old lady with cancer."

"He knows."

"Knows what?"

"What I've been up to. Talking to you guys. Everything."

"You want to expand?"

"Everything."

Dexter was getting irritated with the short answers of Pope. He wanted a concrete plan and Pope wasn't giving it to him. "Pope, please. We need more, a plan. If you want help, give us something. What does Boris want from your mother? Is he using her for some kind of leverage?"

"He's using her, all right."

"For sick shit?"

"No. I mentioned to him once she was an aspiring actress a million years ago. My folks moved out to Hollywood so she could pursue her dreams in acting. She got some commercials and small parts, and things were looking up. Then she got pregnant and had to give up the dream. I'm the reason my mother's acting dreams were crushed."

"Come on, dude. Your mom would trade you for fame? Everyone has dreams that don't come true. I enlisted in the Navy Seals and blew out a knee. Never did one mission. It happens. Mom's still bitter over not making it in Hollywood?"

"She talked about it a lot growing up. Saying how her life would have been different, better, if she had become an actress. Maybe because her marriage to my dad was difficult, or to hurt me. Maybe both?"

"What is Boris using her for?"

"I don't know. But he told me that one day he'd get my mother on the small screen."

"What's the small screen?" John asked, from the back of the SUV.

"TV. I have a suspicion he's using her like he uses all the girls."

"Your mom has cancer. And, not to be mean, is old. Boris

wants young and gullible girls. Your mother doesn't fit the bill."

"I've considered all the variables. Leverage? Boris is a sick guy and trying to make an example out of me by kidnapping Mom. He knows how to jam a knife into your open wounds."

Dexter slumped into the passenger seat of the SUV and watched the cars fly by on the cluttered highway. He reflected on his own family dysfunction and was thinking Pope's issues ran much deeper. Pope's insecurities were created not only by Dad, but now Mom. He worried Pope would do something stupid being in such a fragile state. Pope gripped the steering wheel with one hand and wouldn't look at anyone in the SUV. The highway hypnotized him.

Pope reached with his free hand into the center console and pulled out a pistol. He tossed the gun into his lap and slapped the chamber open to check the ammo.

Full.

"What's the play? We go to Runet hoping Boris and your mom's there? Why not go to the studio if you think he's using her for the small screen?"

"I don't have a play. I'm just preparing for whatever comes our way. We go to Runet, see if Dad's around."

The boys checked their guns. Loaded.

"Is there a way to contact your dad before we find Boris? We should see if he knows something. Maybe he can help us make more of a strategic move," Dexter said, jamming his gun back into his jeans. He could tell Pope was not thinking straight and wasn't in a chatty mood.

"I like Dexter's idea," John said.

Pope dialed up his phone. He waited for an answer. Straight to voicemail.

"No answer. Happy?"

The SUV was only five minutes away from Runet. Dexter was shifting in the passenger seat, thinking of something to convince Pope to make a better plan. He wasn't a fan of reckless attacks when you weren't sure what was in front of you. For being a cowboy, Dexter still had an ounce of common sense, and knew from experience the no-plan-plan made for a lot of unnecessary carnage.

"Call or text your dad again. Tell him we're coming and ask what he knows. I'll feel better," Dexter said.

Pope sighed and resisted picking up his phone which was resting on the center bench. He glanced at Dexter and back at the phone.

He dialed again.

The phone rang a couple times. Voicemail. Pope sent a text and told him to call him back. 911.

"Happy."

"Man of many words. Let's wait to see if your dad calls in the next few minutes. If not, we go with your plan."

"I don't have a plan."

"That's the problem."

John yelled from the backseat because the SUV engine noise was loud as Pope sped on the highway. "Can you tell me about Runet? Is the stuff the Russians are broadcasting internet and web-based only?"

Pope glanced in the rearview mirror and was caught off guard by the question. "How'd you know?"

"The set-up on the hotel TV suggested it. The tour of Runet also confirmed it. And I assume your operation is not being broadcast on local Russian TV. I'm guessing that's not a thing in LA."

"Not enough Russians in LA. Now Hispanics, they

deserve their own channels. But the Russians have a global reach via the internet. They don't need mass media."

John nodded.

Dexter asked. "What is the message these Russians are trying to share? If they only recruit American girls for their work. What is it their exactly trying to propagate to others?"

Pope shrugged. "I don't know how it all works. From what I'm told it's like Netflix. People pay a monthly subscription to access these websites. They can stream these young girls any time they like."

"And you're sure it's not porn?" Dexter asked.

"Not from what I can tell. I had nothing to do with the tech side. I was in recruitment and doing other odd jobs for the organization. That's the confusing part. People apparently pay a lot of money to watch American girls do the news and act in bad sitcoms."

"Sitcoms?"

"Yeah. These girls are wannabe actresses. The organization writes these terrible Netflix original knockoffs and people love it."

"What Russians watch this stuff?"

"All kinds. But once they have their attention, that's how they try to share their message. They do it through the news and other public service announcements."

John scratched his head. "Websites and the internet have IP addresses. These codes are like little address books. Can tell you exactly where the feed is coming from. Also, streaming services from the U.S. rarely work overseas. Maybe Runet is tapping into a market no one else can reach? If they could stream their media across the pond, it would be a goldmine. If you get me a laptop, we can see who's watching this stuff."

Pope glanced into the rearview mirror and raised an

eyebrow at John. Again he was blown away by the intelligence of this country boy from Missouri. He knew more about tech than Pope.

"Impressive John. Surprised you don't have more women beating down your door. You got a sharp mind, my friend."

John rubbed his bloated stomach. "I'm not exactly Fabio. Smarts unfortunately don't equal more dates."

Pope grinned. "I think right now we need to find my dad. We can worry about tech stuff later."

Dexter was glad to hear of a more concrete plan.

The SUV exited the highway and Pope found his way to Runet. By now the afternoon had faded to evening, and the streets were quiet. Skid Row was changing into its night scene. No more casual cars, businesses, or people walking the streets. The darkened streets were now littered with tents and makeshift homes. Men and women huddled around burning trashcans to keep warm.

Pope parked the large vehicle in front of the glass doors to Runet. He jammed the Glock into the back of his jeans and then called his dad one more time.

No answer.

The boys locked and loaded their pistols.

"The streets are different tonight. Is it always like this after dark?"

Pope nodded. "A different world. You don't want to be hanging out here without a buddy, if you know what I mean," Pope checked his phone for the time, "I don't want to make a scene inside Runet. I'll go in first and look for my dad. If I get in trouble, I'll text 911."

The boys nodded.

Dexter turned around and watched the people milling around the streets of Skid Row through the back window of the SUV. He couldn't believe people had to live on the streets. It was such a foreign concept compared to living in rustic LeClaire.

"You hear me, Dexter?" Pope asked, waving his hands in his direction.

"Yeah, sorry, I was distracted. This place is heavy."

"Try to ignore it. I hate to admit this, but when you live around here, you kind of get numb to it. Homeless people become invisible. Not proud of that, but it is what it is," Pope said, pulling out his keys and opening the front doors of Runet, "911, remember? I will find my dad," he said yelling back to the SUV.

The boys nodded and watched Pope disappear into the Runet building. They scanned the dark streets and leaned against the SUV. "So Cal is another planet, right? I can't wait to get home. We need to get this Boris character and take the next train to Clarksville."

"Did you just quote a Monkees lyric?"

"Yeah, so what? They were like the American version of the Beatles. I like their stuff. *Day Dream Believer*, come on?"

"You're too young to like that crap. Besides, The Monkees were actors. It sounds relevant for this crazy town."

John waved off Dexter's comments. "Better than the Johnny Cash crap you listen to. He sounds like a dog with a head cold."

Dexter gave the sign of the cross and pointed to the sky. "Do not disrespect Mr. Cash. He's one of the great music legends of all time."

Before Dexter and John could get in another word and finish their argument, the Runet building lit up. A siren and red lights flashed inside the entrance.

John and Dexter glanced at each other.

"I think that counts as 911," Dexter said.

30

D exter texted Pope to see why the sirens were going off in the building.

No answer.

The glass doors of Runet swung open and dozens of young woman swarmed out into the streets. Three women holding megaphones were yelling at the other ladies and random people walked the streets of Skid Row.

"Run ladies. You're free. Be who God created you to be. Be stars on your own terms."

The woman holding the megaphone looked dirty, like she had been sleeping in the streets. And she had; it was Sylvia who they had met days earlier.

Dexter ran up to Sylvia as more women flocked out of the building. They rushed by him and John, not slowing down or noticing their presence. Most of the women were shouting but not discernible because of the sea of noise.

"What's going on? Where's Jake Pope?" Dexter asked, trying to yell above the shouts.

Sylvia held the megaphone down and glared at Dexter. "How the hell would I know? I hope he's rotting in hell. This isn't about him tonight. This is about women abused and enslaved by Runet. We're setting the captives free."

Sylvia played with a button on the megaphone and cranked up the volume. She even hit a siren button for a second. "Runet is what's wrong with America. Women deserve a voice. And tonight they will have one. No more modern day slavery."

Hordes of woman cheered as they ran into the streets.

John moved away from the angry women and leaned against the SUV. He smiled and enjoyed the beautiful ladies who were now dancing and screaming and flocking into the streets. John thought for a second he should inform the women of his availability, but the timing seemed off.

Dexter leaned down, covered his ears, and yelled above the shouts of Sylvia and the other women. "Can I go inside? I need to find Jake. Did you see Polian?"

"I don't give a shit what you do. Just don't get in our way or you'll get hurt," Sylvia said, giving a raised fist.

Dexter ran into the building as three women dragged a man into the streets. He was bloodied around his nose and his eyes were swollen shut. The women were chanting, "Freedom! Death to the Enemy... Enemy... Enemy..."

The women circled the bloodied man on the sidewalk and continued their chants. Dexter came back for the man, shielded him from more body blows, and told the ladies to back off. The wounded man lay on the sidewalk and writhed in pain. He clutched his ribs and it appeared they had broken his nose.

It was Polian.

Dexter placed his head next to Polian and tried to talk to him above the ruckus of the crowds. "You'll be fine. Did you see Jake inside?"

Polian gave a breathy, *no.*

Dexter waved for John to help Polian into the back of the SUV. At least he'd be safe away from the riled up ladies. He texted Pope again to see if he was okay.

Dexter confronted Sylvia about Polian being beaten half to death. She didn't seem to care. Dexter found it odd that Sylvia was so cold toward Polian. He thought they were friends.

Dexter got on the phone and called Pope instead. No answer. He told John to stay inside the SUV and wait for instructions. Dexter rushed through the glass doors of Runet as the last remnants of the angry women were leaving the building.

The sirens and alarms ceased.

The Runet building was eerily quiet. Lights from the security backups blazed above the door frames. Dexter heard the scampering of feet. He pulled out his pistol and trained it on a staircase that wound up to a second floor. A short blonde women cursed Dexter saying something about freedom, ran down the stairs, and out the front doors.

Dexter smirked and ignored the rude comment.

He yelled for Pope.

Nothing.

Dexter strolled past the receptionist desk. He thought about the girl who sounded like a robot and wanted to be an actress.

He passed the desk and entered the back hallways where Polian gave them the tour. The cubicles where the women worked now empty and headsets lain on small desks.

Dexter called out for Pope again.

Nothing.

The building was silent. No angry women, and no Pope.

Dexter scratched his head and dialed up his phone, not

sure what to do next. "John, it's Dexter. I'm in the building. No sign of Pope. Building is empty. How's Polian?"

John wiped blood from Polian's nose with a rag. "Fine. He'll need some ice and Advil later. Maybe stitches. Those angry chicks did a number on him."

"I'll take one more look around and hope Pope turns up. The building's dark and I have no idea where to go. Maybe Pope's in a back room looking for his dad. He'll be glad we found him, despite looking like he was in a boxing match."

Dexter hung up the phone and jammed it into his back pocket.

He veered right down a row of cubicles and heard a groaning sound. It sounded like someone breathing through a straw. He drew his gun and crept down the aisle near the sound.

"Hello? Pope, is that you?"

Dexter felt a bump at his right boot. He dropped his eyes. A trail of blood was running from his boot to the wall of a cubicle. Pope was propped against it and his breathing was labored.

Pope worked hard to glance up at Dexter. "He's here," Pope said, grasping for breath.

Pope's head was laid to the side and blood was pouring out of his neck. He sucked in air and tried to prop his blonde head of hair with little luck. It sat limp like a noodle. "Boris is here... he shot me..." Pope said, with a cough.

Dexter called John and told him to get an ambulance before Pope bled out.

Dexter yanked out a bandana he kept in his pocket. What he used for what he called snot rockets. He tied the bandana around the neck of Pope and cinched it with his belt. It didn't look pretty but would stop the bleeding until help arrived. "Help's on the way. Where did Boris go?"

Pope nodded toward a door at the end of the aisle of cubicles. Dexter took a deep breath, trained his gun toward the door, and walked for it.

"I'll be back, and hang on. We found your dad, and he's fine."

Pope made no gesture.

31

Dexter's heart pumped blood at a ferocious pace as he neared the metal door. The security light above the exit sign glowed red. Silence. Dexter knew he was walking into a lion's den, not sure where Boris was located.

He flipped down the handle of the metal door and pushed the door open with his boot while keeping the gun high.

It yawned open.

Dexter trained the gun up to the right of a metal staircase that wound out of sight. He heard footfalls on the stairs and yelled into the abyss. "You're done Boris. The authorities are on their way. No way out of this. Come out and I don't put a bullet in your ass."

No response.

Dexter yelled into the swirling staircase, not sure if Boris was on a floor above or somewhere else. Was it even him? He'd hoped the threat would be enough to scare Boris out; not likely.

Dexter slid against the cement wall and eased up the

metal stairs which clapped against his boots. He aimed the gun at a second set of stairs that wound left.

A door slammed shut on the floor above.

His heart was beating in his ears as he ran up the flight of the stairs. Dexter paused at the door on the second floor. Darkness. A rectangular window was on the left side of the door.

Dexter peeked inside.

No sign of life.

He opened the door with his left hand and the gun gripped tightly in his right. He scanned another floor of cubicles. Dexter waved the gun to the left and the right, clearing the area.

Dexter wondered where Pope's mom could've hidden. Was she with Boris? Not likely after Pope being laid down. Unless he wanted Pope's mom to watch Boris put a hole in Jake, always possible.

A voice rang out in the silence. "It's great to meet you, Dexter. I've heard good things about you. Too bad your traitor friend died."

Dexter raised his gun to the ceiling and then back toward the cubicles. He couldn't locate the voice. "Depends how you define traitor. Where I come from anyone who isn't loyal to others is a traitor. You've hurt a lot of people. Maybe you have your categories confused."

The lights inside the building shot on and Dexter shielded his eyes from the brightness.

Boris stood in front of a line of young women. A bank of flat screen TVs were hanging from a back wall behind them. Each girl was sitting in a swivel chair, about six of them. They had gun-shot wounds in their heads. "You see what happens when you deal with traitors?"

Dexter adjusted his eyes from the lights. His stomach

flipped. The aspiring actors were dead. "You're a coward. Only cowards kill young and innocent people."

"This isn't my fault. You can blame your friend Jake, and his incompetent father. It didn't have to come to this. They had a good life working here. But they don't follow orders so well. Just like these women," Boris said, turning to face the dead women slumped in their chairs.

Dexter raised his gun and trained it between Boris' eyes. "Pope's dead. He won't be taking any orders from you any longer. Where's Polian?"

Boris sighed and gave a half grin. "Good... Good... I hope he suffered. Polian is not my problem anymore. He's already taken care of."

"Those girls beat the hell out of him. Was that your doing?"

Boris shrugged.

The screens behind Boris and the dead women lit up. A frail older woman sitting in a chair behind a desk came onto the screen. She glanced down at the desk and then back up to the camera.

Boris said, "In a few minutes the world will know the truth. They will clear my name. And our message will go forth into all the world."

"What message is that? Woman are trash and they deserve to have their dreams crushed? Manipulation? Lying? Murder? Tell me..."

Boris paced in front of the women and waved his gun in the air. "Don't talk like that Mr. O'Kane. You know nothing about my people. We came to this country to pursue the American Dream. Life, liberty, and happiness. America has been good to us. But America is flawed. Our message is needed in this country. Everything I do is to protect this message."

The woman on the TV spoke.

"Show time," Boris said, turning to the screens.

"To whom it may concern," the woman said, giving a weak cough, checking her notes, and glancing back at the cameras.

"I'm shooting this video to stop a very bad man... In 2015, my husband Jim Polian invested in Goldie's Gym. He wanted to partner with the Popov family and bring health and wellness to the Venice Beach area. After a couple years the relationship between Jim and the Popov family soured. Jim, in an act of defiance, laundered money from the Popov family, and committed heinous crimes among the employees, and people associated with their business. I am Jim's wife, but I can't stand by him any longer. He's a criminal and must be dealt with by the authorities. Please contact this number and we will lead you to his whereabouts. I'm sorry for the pain he has caused to the Venice community..."

A tear emerged from the woman's eyes and a phone number blinked on the screen.

Boris had his back turned to Dexter and crossed his arms. He was proud of the work of Mrs. Pope.

Dexter shook his head in disgust. "You lying bastard. That's your play? You pin your crimes on your most loyal followers? You use an old lady with cancer? That doesn't sound powerful to me. Where I come from that move gets your ass kicked no questions asked."

Boris raised his gun at Dexter. He glided toward him. Dexter took a step back and aimed his pistol at Boris.

They locked eyes.

"You think your pathetic video will convince the authorities you're innocent? A little snooping around and LAPD will find everything they need to take you down. A lifetime in prison, or a quick death. Hell is hot, Boris. Go ahead and shoot me, your days are numbered," Dexter said.

The sound of a door squeaking open rang out behind the men. Boris looked past Dexter to see the person walking toward them. "Did you call back up? I knew you couldn't handle this alone," Boris blurted out.

Dexter didn't want to turn around for fear of getting a bullet in the back.

A man limping and walking like a zombie stumbled into the room. A gun hung in his hand next to his limping leg. "So that was your genius move? Use my mom to throw my dad under the bus? Make him suffer because of your crimes? My dad ain't no saint, but you know he was loyal to you. He found out what you were doing and truth hurts. Am I right, Boris?" Pope said, giving a weak cough.

His tee shirt was covered in blood.

"Your dad's weak," Boris said, waving the gun toward Pope, "He was a power hungry man trying to make amends for his sad life. He thought he could take us down with your help. Ha..."

Pope stumbled as the blood loss was causing his vision to blur. He tried to hold his feet steady as the gun wobbled side to side. "I thought you were different. You came alongside me during a hard time. Like a father figure. But you were just using me for your own ends. Those girls were pawns in your sick game. You just wanted money and power and would do anything to get it. I guess everyone has their version of the American Dream."

"Screw you, Pope. You're just noise. Like all the hot air blowing around this town. A failed cop with daddy issues. Not much different from these whores," Boris said, glancing at the dead girls.

Pope raised his gun with all his strength and his eyes

blurred in and out of consciousness. He fought hard to keep his lids open.

Boom.

A stream of blood covered the face of Boris from the hole in his forehead. He dropped to his knees, his mouth opened like he was trying to get in one more word, and he fell into a heap in front of the girls.

Pope turned to see where the bullet came from. Polian came into view. "I needed to do it. I was tired of his talking," Polian said, with a smile. His face was covered in bruises and his dress shirt stained with blood.

"What happened to you?" Pope asked.

"Some girls beat the shit out of me. I deserved it."

Polian glanced at the dead girls in the chairs. He stepped over Boris and knelt down next to one girl. He whispered he was sorry and wished he could've saved them.

"Why did you come in here?" Dexter asked Polian.

"John said he had to do something. He left me in the truck..."

"Figures. Can't follow simple orders. That guy can't sit still for two minutes."

"Where's John now?" Dexter asked.

Polian shrugged.

"Sorry your ex-wife had to get caught up in this junk. How are you going to explain the video to the cops?" Dexter asked Polian.

"I don't know. I'm banking on justice doing its job. They'll see that I was clean and set up by Boris' cronies. Maybe I'll file a kidnapping charge?"

"You guys better get out of here. Not sure what will happen to us, but no sense you getting in trouble. I'll get you guys tickets back to Missouri tonight," Pope said.

Dexter held out a hand to Pope. "I hope things work out.

Hope you find what you're looking for. I know relationships are messy and I should've been more understanding. But you did lie your face off and almost got me killed," Dexter said, with a smirk.

"True. Sorry your first trip to California wasn't more relaxed."

Dexter forced a smile. "I have a lifetime of stories to tell the folks in LeClaire. And I won't be coming back to LA any time soon."

Dexter and John caught the next fight from LA to Kansas City. The guy sitting next to Dexter on the plane had a man-bun. He was from Venice.

32

Dexter and John rested in their seats waiting for the plane to taxi into the terminal at MCI. John leaned over to Dexter and elbowed him in the side.

"I'm disappointed in you."

"What now?"

"When I left Polian in the SUV. You never asked where I went?"

"Wendy's and a Diet Cherry Coke? You can't follow simple orders to save your life."

"Yes, I was hungry. But I didn't go for food. Guess."

"John... I'm tired and don't have time for your games. Did you have to take a leak?"

"Nope. That video Mrs. Pope shot for the Russians. I stopped it from hitting the internet."

"What? How?"

"Remember when I said those IP codes are like little addresses? Well, I put two and two together. I figured whatever crazy stuff the Russians were doing on the internet was fed out of Runet. I used my laptop and found the IP addresses. When I was waiting in the truck, I saw the whole thing on the laptop. Made sure the video never saw the light of day."

"I'll be damned. Your giant head is full of big ole brains. All that wasted time playing with computers in your basement is paying off big guy."

John leaned back in the seat and munched on some peanuts. "Not just a pretty face..."

"Do Polian and Jake know about the video?"

"Yes, sir. Sent them a text. And Polian will get off clean, too."

"How's that?"

"He was convinced his ex-wife was being mistreated at the assisted living facility. He set up a camera in her apartment to check on her. Well, when Boris kidnapped her, it was all on video. Sometimes you need a little luck, or Providence, or something. This will be the last stand for the Russians in Venice."

"Good to hear, can't wait to sleep in my own bed. LA ain't for guys like us. I heard Pope made it through surgery. It seems every time he gets around us he almost dies. I hope everything works out for him and his family. They could use some counseling," Dexter said.

"Speaking of counseling... You smooth things out with Samantha? Is she still pissed at you?"

"She said we could talk tomorrow. We're having lunch."

"Where are you taking her? Somewhere nice?"

"I found a sushi place in the city. I'd like to give raw fish a second chance."

John laughed and slapped Dexter on his head knocking off his John Deere hat. "You can take the country boy out of the country, but ain't no county leaving this cowboy. You getting cultured on me?"

"Don't worry. I've had enough culture in LA to last a lifetime. But those Boston Rolls taste damn good... even with the spicy sauce."

AFTERWORD

In book three of the Antique Assassin series, *Color Blind*, we meet Jake Pope. Pope's an LA cop shipped off to the small town of LeClaire Missouri to work a case with Dexter and John.

I loved bringing back Pope and sending Dexter to L.A. After four books in the series, Dexter and John had not left Missouri, it was time. It's hard to nail down where story ideas come from. But LA needed to be a main character in LA Dreams.

Another reason LA made sense is because that's where I'm from. Maybe I longed for warm weather or ocean breezes now enduring the cold winters of the Midwest, but for whatever reason, it was a ton of fun to write.

Thanks for purchasing another book in the Antique Assassin series and I look forward to writing many more. Will Dexter head to another location outside the confines of LeClaire, who knows?

But it won't be LA any time soon, too crowded. Or will it? Stay tuned and find out...

Cheers,

Ryan J. Pelton
February 2019

HOW TO MAKE AN AUTHOR CRAZY GRATEFUL?

If you liked this book, and want to read more stuff, I can help. And, there are some things you can do that will help me out a ton:

(1) Review the Book

Leave an honest review wherever you purchased this title. You have no idea how that helps me keep writing and publishing. I want to build a rabid tribe of fans that want more of my books. Reviews are essential!

(2) Join the VIP List!

VIP's are what I call the people on my mailing list. They get free books, stories, discounts, updates, and other insider goodies, and, best of all... wait for it, FREE GIVEAWAYS! Visit: ryanjpelton.com.

(3) Try another book

I write tons of stuff (adult fiction, kid's fiction, and nonfiction). Check out my book store: ryanjpelton.-com/book-store.

Thanks for your help, and thanks for reading!

Cheers,

Ryan J. Pelton

www.ingramcontent.com/pod-product-compliance
Lightning Source LLC
Chambersburg PA
CBHW031726170626
46808CB00005B/1907